比较文学与世界文学 研究丛书

主编 曹顺庆

三编 第 **25** 册

李白望月的 150 种方式（上）

张 智 中 著

花木兰文化事业有限公司

国家图书馆出版品预行编目资料

李白望月的 150 种方式（上）／张智中 著 —— 初版 —— 新北市：
花木兰文化事业有限公司，2024〔民 113〕
序 26+ 目 10+222 面；19×26 公分
（比较文学与世界文学研究丛书 三编 第 25 册）
ISBN 978-626-344-824-7（精装）
1.CST：唐诗 2.CST：翻译
810.8   113009378

ISBN-978-626-344-824-7

9 786263 448247

比较文学与世界文学研究丛书
三编 第二五册   ISBN：978-626-344-824-7

李白望月的 150 种方式（上）

作　　者 张智中
主　　编 曹顺庆
企　　划 四川大学双一流学科暨比较文学研究基地
总 编 辑 杜洁祥
副总编辑 杨嘉乐
编辑主任 许郁翎
编　　辑 潘玟静、蔡正宣　美术编辑 陈逸婷
出　　版 花木兰文化事业有限公司
发 行 人 高小娟
联络地址 台湾 235 新北市中和区中安街七二号十三楼
　　　　 电话：02-2923-1455／传真：02-2923-1452
网　　址 http://www.huamulan.tw 信箱 service@huamulans.com
印　　刷 普罗文化出版广告事业
初　　版 2024 年 9 月
定　　价 三编 26 册（精装）新台币 70,000 元
　　　　　　　　　　　　　　　　　　　　版权所有 请勿翻印

李白望月的 150 种方式(上)

张智中 著

作者简介

张智中，南开大学外国语学院教授，博士生导师，翻译系主任，中华诗词外译中心主任、中国翻译协会理事，中国英汉语比较研究会典籍英译专业委员会副会长，《国际诗歌翻译》客座总编，《中国当代诗歌导读》编委会成员。出版编译著 120 余部（专著 6 部），发表论文 120 余篇，获翻译与科研多种奖项。汉诗英译多走向国外，获国际著名诗人和翻译家的广泛好评。译诗观：但为传神，不拘其形，散文笔法，诗意内容；将汉诗英译提高到英诗的高度。

提　　要

　　《李白望月的 150 种方式》是对李白《静夜思》的 150 种英译，均由本书作者独立译出。每种译诗由五个部分组成："读英文"，给出 5-15 个英汉对照的句子，粗体部分是译文中借用或化用的地方；"英文散译"，给出《静夜思》的散文英译；"英文诗译"，在散文英译的基础上，不做任何改动，把散文分行，呈现当代诗歌之形，突出节奏和诗性；"回译"，从"英文诗译"翻译成汉语，并模拟其诗形；"译人语"，是译者的翻译感悟：翻译过程中——包括从《静夜思》到英文译诗，以及从英文译诗到汉语回译——的杂思随想，要言不烦地加以梳理和总结，以阐幽发微，启迪读者。

　　本书之创新，概有三点：其一，以一人之力，译出《静夜思》150 余种或繁或简或浓或淡不同风格的版本，可证诗歌可译，而且，诗可多译；其二，阅读英文，并借鉴入诗或译诗，不仅可提升译诗的质量，还可激发译者的想象力，致译诗意象丰盈，意境涵咏。其三，译者的译诗理念，受到央视《经典咏流传》和解构主义翻译观的影响，不求语言表层的忠实，重在深层诗意的挖掘与再现。

　　总之，本书恰好体现了译者的译诗理念："但为传神，不拘其形，散文笔法，诗意内容"，以达"将汉诗英译提高到英诗的高度"之目的。本书为读者提供全新的阅读视角，为诗歌的翻译和创作提供有益的参考和启示。

静夜思

李白

床前明月光，
疑是地上霜。
举头望明月，
低头思故乡。

东方之月，皎兮。
Oh, bright is the moon, the Oriental moon.

都是月亮惹的祸。
The moon as an inducer of nostalgia.

梵译千篇广，归心一念生。
（宋．鲍当《送白上人归天台》）
A prolific translator as a recluse,
or moon-gazer.

比较文学的中国路径

曹顺庆

自德国作家歌德提出"世界文学"观念以来，比较文学已经走过近二百年。比较文学研究也历经欧洲阶段、美洲阶段而至亚洲阶段，并在每一阶段都形成了独具特色学科理论体系、研究方法、研究范围及研究对象。中国比较文学研究面对东西文明之间不断加深的交流和碰撞现况，立足中国之本，辩证吸纳四方之学，而有了如今欣欣向荣之景象，这套丛书可以说是应运而生。本丛书尝试以开放性、包容性分批出版中国比较文学学者研究成果，以观中国比较文学学术脉络、学术理念、学术话语、学术目标之概貌。

一、百年比较文学争讼之端——比较文学的定义

什么是比较文学？常识告诉我们：比较文学就是文学比较。然而当今中国比较文学教学实际情况却并非完全如此。长期以来，中国学术界对"什么是比较文学？"却一直说不清，道不明。这一最基本的问题，几乎成为学术界纠缠不清、莫衷一是的陷阱，存在着各种不同的看法。其中一些看法严重误导了广大学生！如果不辨析这些严重误导了广大学生的观点，是不负责任、问心有愧的。恰如《文心雕龙·序志》说"岂好辩哉，不得已也"，因此我不得不辩。

其中一个极为容易误导学生的说法，就是"比较文学不是文学比较"。目前，一些教科书郑重其事地指出：比较文学不是文学比较。认为把"比较"与"文学"联系在一起，很容易被人们理解为用比较的方法进行文学研究的意思。并进一步强调，比较文学并不等于文学比较，并非任何运用比较方法来进行的比较研究都是比较文学。这种误导学生的说法几乎成为一个定论，

一个基本常识，其实，这个看法是不完全准确的。

让我们来看看一些具体例证，请注意，我列举的例证，对事不对人，因而不提及具体的人名与书名，请大家理解。在 Y 教授主编的教材中，专门设有一节以"比较文学不是文学比较"为题的内容，其中指出"比较文学界面临的最大的困惑就是把'比较文学'误读为'文学比较'"，在高等院校进行比较文学课程教学时需要重点强调"比较文学不是文学比较"。W 教授主编的教材也称"比较文学不是文学的比较"，因为"不是所有用比较的方法来研究文学现象的都是比较文学"。L 教授在其所著教材专门谈到"比较文学不等于文学比较"，因为，"比较"已经远远超出了一般方法论的意义，而具有了跨国家与民族、跨学科的学科性质，认为将比较文学等同于文学比较是以偏概全的。"J 教授在其主编的教材中指出，"比较文学并不等于文学比较"，并以美国学派雷马克的比较文学定义为根据，论证比较文学的"比较"是有前提的，只有在地域观念上跨越打通国家的界限，在学科领域上跨越打通文学与其他学科的界限，进行的比较研究才是比较文学。在 W 教授主编的教材中，作者认为，"若把比较文学精神看作比较精神的话，就是犯了望文生义的错误，一百余年来，比较文学这个名称是名不副实的。"

从列举的以上教材我们可以看出，首先，它们在当下都仍然坚持"比较文学不是文学比较"这一并不完全符合整个比较文学学科发展事实的观点。如果认为一百余年来，比较文学这个名称是名不副实的，所有的比较文学都不是文学比较，那是大错特错！其次，值得注意的是，这些教材在相关叙述中各自的侧重点还并不相同，存在着不同程度、不同方面的分歧。这样一来，错误的观点下多样的谬误解释，加剧了学习者对比较文学学科性质的错误把握，使得学习者对比较文学的理解愈发困惑，十分不利于比较文学方法论的学习、也不利于比较文学学科的传承和发展。当今中国比较文学教材之所以普遍出现以上强作解释，不完全准确的教科书观点，根本原因还是没有仔细研究比较文学学科不同阶段之史实，甚至是根本不清楚比较文学不同阶段的学科史实的体现。

实际上，早期的比较文学"名"与"实"的确不相符合，这主要是指法国学派的学科理论，但是并不包括以后的美国学派及中国学派的学科理论，如果把所有阶段的学科理论一锅煮，是不妥当的。下面，我们就从比较文学学科发展的史实来论证这个问题。"比较文学不是文学比较""comparative literature is not literary comparison"，只是法国学派提出的比较文学口号，只是法国学派一派的主张，而不是整个比较文学学科的基本特征。我们不能够把这个阶段性的比较文学口号扩大化，甚至让其突破时空，用于描述比较文学所有的阶段和学派，更不能够使其"放之四海而皆准"。

法国学派提出"比较文学不是文学比较"，这个"比较"（comparison）是他们坚决反对的！为什么呢，因为他们要的不是文学"比较"（literary comparison），而是文学"关系"（literary relationship），具体而言，他们主张比较文学是实证的国际文学关系，是不同国家文学的影响关系，influences of different literatures，而不是文学比较。

法国学派为什么要反对"比较"（comparison），这与比较文学第一次危机密切相关。比较文学刚刚在欧洲兴起时，难免泥沙俱下，乱比的情形不断出现，暴露了多种隐患和弊端，于是，其合法性遭到了学者们的质疑：究竟比较文学的科学性何在？意大利著名美学大师克罗齐认为，"比较"（comparison）是各个学科都可以应用的方法，所以，"比较"不能成为独立学科的基石。学术界对于比较文学公然的质疑与挑战，引起了欧洲比较文学学者的震撼，到底比较文学如何"比较"才能够避免"乱比"？如何才是科学的比较？

难能可贵的是，法国学者对于比较文学学科的科学性进行了深刻的的反思和探索，并提出了具体的应对的方法：法国学派采取壮士断臂的方式，砍掉"比较"（comparison），提出比较文学不是文学比较（comparative literature is not literary comparison），或者说砍掉了没有影响关系的平行比较，总结出了只注重文学关系（literary relationship）的影响（influences）研究方法论。法国学派的创建者之一基亚指出，比较文学并不是比较。比较不过是一门名字没取好的学科所运用的一种方法……企图对它的性质下一个严格的定义可能是徒劳的。基亚认为：比较文学不是平行比较，而仅仅是文学关系史。以"文学关系"为比较文学研究的正宗。为什么法国学派要反对比较？或者说为什么法国学派要提出"比较文学不是文学比较"，因为法国学派认为"比较"（comparison）实际上是乱比的根源，或者说"比较"是没有可比性的。正如巴登斯佩哲指出："仅仅对两个不同的对象同时看上一眼就作比较，仅仅靠记忆和印象的拼凑，靠一些主观臆想把可能游移不定的东西扯在一起来找点类似点，这样的比较决不可能产生论证的明晰性"。所以必须抛弃"比较"。只承认基于科学的历史实证主义之上的文学影响关系研究（based on scientificity and positivism and literary influences.)。法国学派的代表学者卡雷指出：比较文学是实证性的关系研究："比较文学是文学史的一个分支：它研究拜伦与普希金、歌德与卡莱尔、瓦尔特·司各特与维尼之间，在属于一种以上文学背景的不同作品、不同构思以及不同作家的生平之间所曾存在过的跨国度的精神交往与实际联系。"正因为法国学者善于独辟蹊径，敢于提出"比较文学不是文学比较"，甚至完全抛弃比较（comparison），以防止"乱比"，才形成了一套建立在"科学"实证性为基础的、以影响关系为特征的"不比较"的比较文学学科理论体系，这终于挡住了克罗齐等人对比较文学"乱比"的批判，形成了以"科学"实证为特征的文学影响关系研究，确立了法国学派的学科理论和一整套方法论体系。当然，法国学派悍然砍掉比较研究，又不放弃"比较文学"这个名称，于是不可避免地出现了比较文学名不副实的尴尬现象，出现了打着比较文学名号，而又不比较的法国学派学科理论，这才是问题的关键。

当然，法国学派提出"比较文学不是文学比较"，只注重实证关系而不注重文学比较和文学审美，必然会引起比较文学的危机。这一危机终于由美国著名比较文学家韦勒克（René Wellek）在 1958 年国际比较文学协会第二次大会上明确揭示出来了。在这届年会上，韦勒克作了题为《比较文学的危机》的挑战性发言，对"不比较"的法国学派进行了猛烈批判，宣告了倡导平行比较和注重文学审美的比较文学美国学派的诞生。韦勒克作了题为《比较文学的危机》的挑战性发言，对当时一统天下的法国学派进行了猛烈批判，宣告了比较文学美国学派的诞生。韦勒克说："我认为，内容和方法之间的人为界线，渊源和影响的机械主义概念，以及尽管是十分慷慨的但仍属文化民族主义的动机，是比较文学研究中持久危机的症状。"韦勒克指出："比较也不能仅仅局限在历史上的事实联系中，正如最近语言学家的经验向文学研究者表明的那样，比较的价值既存在于事实联系的影响研究中，也存在于毫无历史关系的语言现象或类型的平等对比中。"很明显，韦勒克提出了比较文学就是要比较（comparison），就是要恢复巴登斯佩哲所讽刺和抛弃的"找点类似点"的平行比较研究。美国著名比较文学家雷马克（Henry Remak）在他的著名论文《比较文学的定义与功用》中深刻地分析了法国学派为什么放弃"比较"（comparison）的原因和本质。他分析说："法国比较文学否定'纯粹'的比较（comparison），它忠实于十九世纪实证主义学术研究的传统，即实证主义所坚持并热切期望的文学研究的'科学性'。按照这种观点，纯粹的类比不会得出任何结论，尤其是不能得出有更大意义的、系统的、概括性的结论。……既然值得尊重的科学必须致力于因果关系的探索，而比较文学必须具有科学性，因此，比较文学应该研究因果关系，即影响、交流、变更等。"雷马克进一步尖锐地指出，"比较文学"不是"影响文学"。只讲影响不要比较的"比较文学"，当然是名不副实的。显然，法国学派抛弃了"比较"（comparison），但是仍然带着一顶"比较文学"的帽子，才造成了比较文学"名"与"实"不相符合，造成比较文学不比较的尴尬，这才是问题的关键。

美国学派最大的贡献，是恢复了被法国学派所抛弃的比较文学应有的本义——"比较"（The American school went back to the original sense of comparative literature ——"comparison"），美国学派提出了标志其学派学科理论体系的平行比较和跨学科比较："比较文学是一国文学与另一国或多国文学的比较，是文学与人类其他表现领域的比较。"显然，自从美国学派倡导比较文学应当比较（comparison）以后，比较文学就不再有名与实不相符合的问题了，我们就不应当再继续笼统地说"比较文学不是文学比较"了，不应当再以"比较文学不是文学比较"来误导学生！更不可以说"一百余年来，比较文学这个名称是名不副实的。"不能够将雷马克的观点也强行解释为"比较文学不是比较"。因为在美国学派看来，比较文学就是要比较（comparison）。比较文学就是要恢复被巴登斯佩哲所讽刺和抛弃的"找点类似点"的平行比较研究。因为平行研究的可比性，正是类同性。正如韦勒克所说，"比较的价值既存在于事实联系的影响研究中，也存在于毫无历史关系的语言现象或类型的平等对比中。"恢复平行比较研究、跨学科研究，形成了以"找点类似点"的平行研究和跨学科研究为特征的比较文学美国学派学科理论和方法论体系。美国学派的学科理论以"类型学"、"比较诗学"、"跨学科比较"为主，并拓展原属于影响研究的"主题学"、"文类学"等领域，大大扩展比较文学研究领域。

二、比较文学的三个阶段

下面，我们从比较文学的三个学科理论阶段，进一步剖析比较文学不同阶段的学科理论特征。现代意义上的比较文学学科发展以"跨越"与"沟通"为目标，形成了类似"层叠"式、"涟漪"式的发展模式，经历了三个重要的学科理论阶段，即：

一、欧洲阶段，比较文学的成形期；二、美洲阶段，比较文学的转型期；三、亚洲阶段，比较文学的拓展期。我们将比较文学三个阶段的发展称之为"涟漪式"结构，实际上是揭示了比较文学学科理论的继承与创新的辩证关系：比较文学学科理论的发展，不是以新的理论否定和取代先前的理论，而是层叠式、累进式地形成"涟漪"式的包容性发展模式，逐步积累推进。比较文学学科理论发展呈现为层叠式、"涟漪"式、包容式的发展模式。我们把这个模式描绘如下：

法国学派主张比较文学是国际文学关系，是不同国家文学的影响关系。形成学科理论第一圈层：比较文学——影响研究；美国学派主张恢复平行比较，形成学科理论第二圈层：比较文学——影响研究＋平行研究＋跨学科研究；中国学派提出跨文明研究和变异研究，形成学科理论第三圈层：比较文学——影响研究＋平行研究＋跨学科研究＋跨文明研究＋变异研究。这三个圈层并不互相排斥和否定，而是继承和包容。我们将比较文学三个阶段的发展称之为层叠式、"涟漪"式、包容式结构，实际上是揭示了比较文学学科理论的继承与创新的辩证关系。

法国学派提出，可比性的第一个立足点是同源性，由关系构成的同源性。同源性主要是针对影响关系研究而言的。法国学派将同源性视作可比性的核心，认为影响研究的可比性是同源性。所谓同源性，指的是通过对不同国家、不同民族和不同语言的文学的文学关系研究，寻求一种有事实联系的同源关系，这种影响的同源关系可以通过直接、具体的材料得以证实。同源性往往建立在一条可追溯关系的三点一线的"影响路线"之上，这条路线由发送者、接受者和传递者三部分构成。如果没有相同的源流，也就不可能有影响关系，也就谈不上可比性，这就是"同源性"。以渊源学、流传学和媒介学作为研究的中心，依靠具体的事实材料在国别文学之间寻求主题、题材、文体、原型、思想渊源等方面的同源影响关系。注重事实性的关联和渊源性的影响，并采用严谨的实证方法，重视对史料的搜集和求证，具有重要的学术价值与学术意义，仍然具有广阔的研究前景。渊源学的例子：杨宪益，《西方十四行诗的渊源》。

比较文学学科理论的第二阶段在美洲，第二阶段是比较文学学科理论的转型期。从 20 世纪 60 年代以来，比较文学研究的主要阵地逐渐从法国转向美国，平行研究的可比性是什么？是类同性。类同性是指是没有文学影响关系的不同国家文学所表现出的相似和契合之处。以类同性为基本立足点的平行研究与影响研究一样都是超出国界的文学研究，但它不涉及影响关系研究的放送、流传、媒介等问题。平行研究强调不同国家的作家、作品、文学现象的类同比较，比较结果是总结出于文学作品的美学价值及文学发展具有规律性的东西。其比较必须具有可比性，这个可比性就是类同性。研究文学中类同的：风格、结构、内容、形式、流派、情节、技巧、手法、情调、形象、主题、文类、文学思潮、文学理论、文学规律。例如钱钟书《通感》认为，中国诗文有一种描写手法，古代批评家和修辞学家似乎都没有拈出。宋祁《玉楼春》词有句名句："红杏枝头春意闹。"这与西方的通感描写手法可以比较。

比较文学的又一次危机：比较文学的死亡

九十年代，欧美学者提出，比较文学作为一门学科已经死亡！最早是英国学者苏珊·巴斯奈特1993年她在《比较文学》一书中提出了比较文学的死亡论，认为比较文学作为一门学科，在某种意义上已经死亡。尔后，美国学者斯皮瓦克写了一部比较文学专著，书名就叫《一个学科的死亡》。为什么比较文学会死亡，斯皮瓦克的书中并没有明确回答！为什么西方学者会提出比较文学死亡论？全世界比较文学界都十分困惑。我们认为，20世纪90年代以来，欧美比较文学继"理论热"之后，又出现了大规模的"文化转向"。脱离了比较文学的基本立场。首先是不比较，即不讲比较文学的可比性问题。西方比较文学研究充斥大量的 Culture Studies（文化研究），已经不考虑比较的合理性，不考虑比较文学的可比性问题。第二是不文学，即不关心文学问题。西方学者热衷于文化研究，关注的已经不是文学性，而是精神分析、政治、性别、阶级、结构等等。最根本的原因，是比较文学学科长期囿于西方中心论，有意无意地回避东西方不同文明文学的比较问题，基本上忽略了学科理论的新生长点，比较文学学科理论缺乏创新，严重忽略了比较文学的差异性和变异性。

要克服比较文学的又一次危机，就必须打破西方中心论，克服比较文学学科理论一味求同的比较文学学科理论模式，提出适应当今全球化比较文学研究的新话语。中国学派，正是在此次危机中，提出了比较文学变异学研究，总结出了新的学科理论话语和一套新的方法论。

中国大陆第一部比较文学概论性著作是卢康华、孙景尧所著《比较文学导论》，该书指出："什么是比较文学？现在我们可以借用我国学者季羡林先生的解释来回答了：'顾名思义，比较文学就是把不同国家的文学拿出来比较，这可以说是狭义的比较文学。广义的比较文学是把文学同其他学科来比较，包括人文科学和社会科学'。"[1]这个定义可以说是美国雷马克定义的翻版。不过，该书又接着指出："我们认为最精炼易记的还是我国学者钱钟书先生的说法：'比较文学作为一门专门学科，则专指跨越国界和语言界限的文学比较'。更具体地说，就是把不同国家不同语言的文学现象放在一起进行比较，研究他们在文艺理论、文学思潮，具体作家、作品之间的互相影响。"[2]这个定义似乎更接近法国学派的定义，没有强调平行比较与跨学科比较。紧接该书之后的教材是陈挺的《比较文学简编》，该书仍旧以"广义"与"狭义"来解释比较文学的定义，指出："我们认为，通常说的比较文学是狭义的，即指超越国家、民族和语言界限的文学研究……广义的比较文学还可以包括文学与其他艺术（音乐、绘画等）与其他意识形态（历史、哲学、政治、宗教等）之间的相互关系的研究。"[3]中国比较文学早期对于比较文学的定义中凸显了很强的不确定性。

由乐黛云主编，高等教育出版社 1988 年的《中西比较文学教程》，则对比较文学定义有了较为深入的认识，该书在详细考查了中外不同的定义之后，该书指出："比较文学不应受到语言、民族、国家、学科等限制，而要走向一种开放性，力图寻求世界文学发展的共同规律。"[4]"世界文学"概念的纳入极大拓宽了比较文学的内涵，为"跨文化"定义特征的提出做好了铺垫。

随着时间的推移，学界的认识逐步深化。1997 年，陈惇、孙景尧、谢天振主编的《比较文学》提出了自己的定义："把比较文学看作跨民族、跨语言、跨文化、跨学科的文学研究，更符合比较文学的实质，更能反映现阶段人们对于比较文学的认识。"[5]2000 年北京师范大学出版社出版了《比较文学概论》修订本，提出："什么是比较文学呢？比较文学是一种开放式的文学研究，它具有宏观的视野和国际的角度，以跨民族、跨语言、跨文化、跨学科界限的各种文学关系为研究对象，在理论和方法上，具有比较的自觉意识和兼容并包的特色。"[6]这是我们目前所看到的国内较有特色的一个定义。

---

1 卢康华、孙景尧著《比较文学导论》，黑龙江人民出版社 1984，第 15 页。
2 卢康华、孙景尧著《比较文学导论》，黑龙江人民出版社 1984 年版。
3 陈挺《比较文学简编》，华东师范大学出版社 1986 年版。
4 乐黛云主编《中西比较文学教程》，高等教育出版社 1988 年版。
5 陈惇、孙景尧、谢天振主编《比较文学》，高等教育出版社 1997 年版。
6 陈惇、刘象愚《比较文学概论》，北京师范大学出版社 2000 年版。

具有代表性的比较文学定义是 2002 年出版的杨乃乔主编的《比较文学概论》一书，该书的定义如下："比较文学是以跨民族、跨语言、跨文化与跨学科为比较视域而展开的研究，在学科的成立上以研究主体的比较视域为安身立命的本体，因此强调研究主体的定位，同时比较文学把学科的研究客体定位于民族文学之间与文学及其他学科之间的三种关系：材料事实关系、美学价值关系与学科交叉关系，并在开放与多元的文学研究中追寻体系化的汇通。"[7]方汉文则认为："比较文学作为文学研究的一个分支学科，它以理解不同文化体系和不同学科间的同一性和差异性的辩证思维为主导，对那些跨越了民族、语言、文化体系和学科界限的文学现象进行比较研究，以寻求人类文学发生和发展的相似性和规律性。"[8]由此而引申出的"跨文化"成为中国比较文学学者对于比较文学定义所做出的历史性贡献。

我在《比较文学教程》中对比较文学定义表述如下："比较文学是以世界性眼光和胸怀来从事不同国家、不同文明和不同学科之间的跨越式文学比较研究。它主要研究各种跨越中文学的同源性、变异性、类同性、异质性和互补性，以影响研究、变异研究、平行研究、跨学科研究、总体文学研究为基本方法论，其目的在于以世界性眼光来总结文学规律和文学特性，加强世界文学的相互了解与整合，推动世界文学的发展。"[9]在这一定义中，我再次重申"跨国""跨学科""跨文明"三大特征，以"变异性""异质性"突破东西文明之间的"第三堵墙"。

"首在审己，亦必知人"。中国比较文学学者在前人定义的不断论争中反观自身，立足中国经验、学术传统，以中国学者之言为比较文学的危机处境贡献学科转机之道。

三、两岸共建比较文学话语——比较文学中国学派

中国学者对于比较文学定义的不断明确也促成了"比较文学中国学派"的生发。得益于两岸几代学者的垦拓耕耘，这一议题成为近五十年来中国比较文学发展中竖起的最鲜明、最具争议性的一杆大旗，同时也是中国比较文学学科理论研究最有创新性，最亮丽的一道风景线。

7 杨乃乔主编《比较文学概论》，北京大学出版社 2002 年版。
8 方汉文《比较文学基本原理》，苏州大学出版社 2002 年版。
9 曹顺庆《比较文学教程》，高等教育出版社 2006 年版。

比较文学"中国学派"这一概念所蕴含的理论的自觉意识最早出现的时间大约是 20 世纪 70 年代。当时的台湾由于派出学生留洋学习，接触到大量的比较文学学术动态，率先掀起了中外文学比较的热潮。1971 年 7 月在台湾淡江大学召开的第一届"国际比较文学会议"上，朱立元、颜元叔、叶维廉、胡辉恒等学者在会议期间提出了比较文学的"中国学派"这一学术构想。同时，李达三、陈鹏翔（陈慧桦）、古添洪等致力于比较文学中国学派早期的理论催生。如 1976 年，古添洪、陈慧桦出版了台湾比较文学论文集《比较文学的垦拓在台湾》。编者在该书的序言中明确提出："我们不妨大胆宣言说，这援用西方文学理论与方法并加以考验、调整以用之于中国文学的研究，是比较文学中的中国派"[10]。这是关于比较文学中国学派较早的说明性文字，尽管其中提到的研究方法过于强调西方理论的普世性，而遭到美国和中国大陆比较文学学者的批评和否定；但这毕竟是第一次从定义和研究方法上对中国学派的本质进行了系统论述，具有开拓和启明的作用。后来，陈鹏翔又在台湾《中外文学》杂志上连续发表相关文章，对自己提出的观点作了进一步的阐释和补充。

在"中国学派"刚刚起步之际，美国学者李达三起到了启蒙、催生的作用。李达三于 60 年代来华在台湾任教，为中国比较文学培养了一批朝气蓬勃的生力军。1977 年 10 月，李达三在《中外文学》6 卷 5 期上发表了一篇宣言式的文章《比较文学中国学派》，宣告了比较文学的中国学派的建立，并认为比较文学中国学派旨在"与比较文学中早已定于一尊的西方思想模式分庭抗礼。由于这些观念是源自对中国文学及比较文学有兴趣的学者，我们就将含有这些观念的学者统称为比较文学的'中国'学派。"并指出中国学派的三个目标：1、在自己本国的文学中，无论是理论方面或实践方面，找出特具"民族性"的东西，加以发扬光大，以充实世界文学；2、推展非西方国家"地区性"的文学运动，同时认为西方文学仅是众多文学表达方式之一而已；3、做一个非西方国家的发言人，同时并不自诩能代表所有其他非西方的国家。李达三后来又撰文对比较文学研究状况进行了分析研究，积极推动中国学派的理论建设。[11]

继中国台湾学者垦拓之功，在 20 世纪 70 年代末复苏的大陆比较文学研

10 古添洪、陈慧桦《比较文学的垦拓在台湾》，台湾东大图书公司 1976 年版。
11 李达三《比较文学研究之新方向》，台湾联经事业出版公司 1978 年版。

究亦积极参与了"比较文学中国学派"的理论建设和学科建设。

　　季羡林先生 1982 年在《比较文学译文集》的序言中指出："以我们东方文学基础之雄厚，历史之悠久，我们中国文学在其中更占有独特的地位，只要我们肯努力学习，认真钻研，比较文学中国学派必然能建立起来，而且日益发扬光大"[12]。1983 年 6 月，在天津召开的新中国第一次比较文学学术会议上，朱维之先生作了题为《比较文学中国学派的回顾与展望》的报告，在报告中他旗帜鲜明地说："比较文学中国学派的形成（不是建立）已经有了长远的源流，前人已经做出了很多成绩，颇具特色，而且兼有法、美、苏学派的特点。因此，中国学派绝不是欧美学派的尾巴或补充"[13]。1984 年，卢康华、孙景尧在《比较文学导论》中对如何建立比较文学中国学派提出了自己的看法，认为应当以马克思主义作为自己的理论基础，以我国的优秀传统与民族特色为立足点与出发点，汲取古今中外一切有用的营养，去努力发展中国的比较文学研究。同年在《中国比较文学》创刊号上，朱维之、方重、唐弢、杨周翰等人认为中国的比较文学研究应该保持不同于西方的民族特点和独立风貌。1985 年，黄宝生发表《建立比较文学的中国学派：读〈中国比较文学〉创刊号》，认为《中国比较文学》创刊号上多篇讨论比较文学中国学派的论文标志着大陆对比较文学中国学派的探讨进入了实际操作阶段。[14]1988 年，远浩一提出"比较文学是跨文化的文学研究"（载《中国比较文学》1988 年第 3 期）。这是对比较文学中国学派在理论特征和方法论体系上的一次前瞻。同年，杨周翰先生发表题为"比较文学：界定'中国学派'，危机与前提"（载《中国比较文学通讯》1988 年第 2 期），认为东方文学之间的比较研究应当成为"中国学派"的特色。这不仅打破比较文学中的欧洲中心论，而且也是东方比较学者责无旁贷的任务。此外，国内少数民族文学的比较研究，也应该成为"中国学派"的一个组成部分。所以，杨先生认为比较文学中的大量问题和学派问题并不矛盾，相反有助于理论的讨论。1990 年，远浩一发表"关于'中国学派'"（载《中国比较文学》1990 年第 1 期），进一步推进了"中国学派"的研究。此后直到 20 世纪 90 年代末，中国学者就比较文学中国学派的建立、理论与方法以及相应的学科理论等诸多问题进行了积极而富有成效的探讨。

---

12 张隆溪《比较文学译文集》，北京大学出版社 1984 年版。

13 朱维之《比较文学论文集》，南开大学出版社 1984 年版。

14 参见《世界文学》1985 年第 5 期。

刘介民、远浩一、孙景尧、谢天振、陈淳、刘象愚、杜卫等人都对这些问题付出过不少努力。《暨南学报》1991 年第 3 期发表了一组笔谈，大家就这个问题提出了意见，认为必须打破比较文学研究中长期存在的法美研究模式，建立比较文学中国学派的任务已经迫在眉睫。王富仁在《学术月刊》1991 年第 4 期上发表"论比较文学的中国学派问题"，论述中国学派兴起的必然性。而后，以谢天振等学者为代表的比较文学研究界展开了对"X+Y"模式的批判。比较文学在大陆复兴之后，一些研究者采取了"X+Y"式的比附研究的模式，在发现了"惊人的相似"之后便万事大吉，而不注意中西巨大的文化差异性，成为了浅度的比附性研究。这种情况的出现，不仅是中国学者对比较文学的理解上出了问题，也是由于法美学派研究理论中长期存在的研究模式的影响，一些学者并没有深思中国与西方文学背后巨大的文明差异性，因而形成"X+Y"的研究模式，这更促使一些学者思考比较文学中国学派的问题。

经过学者们的共同努力，比较文学中国学派一些初步的特征和方法论体系逐渐凸显出来。1995 年，我在《中国比较文学》第 1 期上发表《比较文学中国学派基本理论特征及其方法论体系初探》一文，对比较文学在中国复兴十余年来的发展成果作了总结，并在此基础上总结出中国学派的理论特征和方法论体系，对比较文学中国学派作了全方位的阐述。继该文之后，我又发表了《跨越第三堵'墙'创建比较文学中国学派理论体系》等系列论文，论述了以跨文化研究为核心的"中国学派"的基本理论特征及其方法论体系。这些学术论文发表之后在国内外比较文学界引起了较大的反响。台湾著名比较文学学者古添洪认为该文"体大思精，可谓已综合了台湾与大陆两地比较文学中国学派的策略与指归，实可作为'中国学派'在大陆再出发与实践的蓝图"[15]。

在我撰文提出比较文学中国学派的基本特征及方法论体系之后，关于中国学派的论争热潮日益高涨。反对者如前国际比较文学学会会长佛克马（Douwe Fokkema）1987 年在中国比较文学学会第二届学术讨论会上就从所谓的国际观点出发对比较文学中国学派的合法性提出了质疑，并坚定地反对建立比较文学中国学派。来自国际的观点并没有让中国学者失去建立比较文学中国学派的热忱。很快中国学者智量先生就在《文艺理论研究》1988 年第

---

15 古添洪《中国学派与台湾比较文学界的当前走向》，参见黄维梁编《中国比较文学理论的垦拓》167 页，北京大学出版社 1998 年版。

1 期上发表题为《比较文学在中国》一文，文中援引中国比较文学研究取得的成就，为中国学派辩护，认为中国比较文学研究成绩和特色显著，尤其在研究方法上足以与比较文学研究历史上的其他学派相提并论，建立中国学派只会是一个有益的举动。1991 年，孙景尧先生在《文学评论》第 2 期上发表《为"中国学派"一辩》，孙先生认为佛克马所谓的国际主义观点实质上是"欧洲中心主义"的观点，而"中国学派"的提出，正是为了清除东西方文学与比较文学学科史中形成的"欧洲中心主义"。在 1993 年美国印第安纳大学举行的全美比较文学会议上，李达三仍然坚定地认为建立中国学派是有益的。二十年之后，佛克马教授修正了自己的看法，在 2007 年 4 月的"跨文明对话——国际学术研讨会（成都）"上，佛克马教授公开表示欣赏建立比较文学中国学派的想法[16]。即使学派争议一派繁荣景象，但最终仍旧需要落点于学术创见与成果之上。

比较文学变异学便是中国学派的一个重要理论创获。2005 年，我正式在《比较文学学》[17]中提出比较文学变异学，提出比较文学研究应该从"求同"思维中走出来，从"变异"的角度出发，拓宽比较文学的研究。通过前述的法、美学派学科理论的梳理，我们也可以发现前期比较文学学科是缺乏"变异性"研究的。我便从建构中国比较文学学科理论话语体系入手，立足《周易》的"变异"思想，建构起"比较文学变异学"新话语，力图以中国学者的视角为全世界比较文学学科理论提供一个新视角、新方法和新理论。

比较文学变异学的提出根植于中国哲学的深层内涵，如《周易》之"易之三名"所构建的"变易、简易、不易"三位一体的思辨意蕴与意义生成系统。具体而言，"变易"乃四时更替、五行运转、气象畅通、生生不息；"不易"乃天上地下、君南臣北、纲举目张、尊卑有位；"简易"则是乾以易知、坤以简能、易则易知、简则易从。显然，在这个意义结构系统中，变易强调"变"，不易强调"不变"，简易强调变与不变之间的基本关联。万物有所变，有所不变，且变与不变之间存在简单易从之规律，这是一种思辨式的变异模式，这种变异思维的理论特征就是：天人合一、物我不分、对立转化、整体关联。这是中国古代哲学最重要的认识论，也是与西方哲学所不同的"变异"思想。

---

16 见《比较文学报》2007 年 5 月 30 日，总第 43 期。
17 曹顺庆《比较文学学》，四川大学出版社 2005 年版。

由哲学思想衍生于学科理论，比较文学变异学是"指对不同国家、不同文明的文学现象在影响交流中呈现出的变异状态的研究，以及对不同国家、不同文明的文学相互阐发中出现的变异状态的研究。通过研究文学现象在影响交流以及相互阐发中呈现的变异，探究比较文学变异的规律。"[18]变异学理论的重点在求"异"的可比性，研究范围包含跨国变异研究、跨语际变异研究、跨文化变异研究、跨文明变异研究、文学的他国化研究等方面。比较文学变异学所发现的文化创新规律、文学创新路径是基于中国所特有的术语、概念和言说体系之上探索出的"中国话语"，作为比较文学第三阶段中国学派的代表性理论已经受到了国际学界的广泛关注与高度评价，中国学术话语产生了世界性影响。

四、国际视野中的中国比较文学

文明之墙让中国比较文学学者所提出的标识性概念获得国际视野的接纳、理解、认同以及运用，经历了跨语言、跨文化、跨文明的多重关卡，国际视野下的中国比较文学书写亦经历了一个从"遍寻无迹""只言片语"而"专篇专论"，从最初的"话语乌托邦"至"阶段性贡献"的过程。

二十世纪六十年代以来港台学者致力于从课程教学、学术平台、人才培养，国内外学术合作等方面巩固比较文学这一新兴学科的建立基石，如淡江文理学院英文系开设的"比较文学"（1966），香港大学开设的"中西文学关系"（1966）等课程；台湾大学外文系主编出版之《中外文学》月刊、淡江大学出版之《淡江评论》季刊等比较文学研究专刊；后又有台湾比较文学学会（1973 年）、香港比较文学学会（1978）的成立。在这一系列的学术环境构建下，学者前贤以"中国学派"为中国比较文学话语核心在国际比较文学学科理论、方法论中持续探讨，率先启声。例如李达三在 1980 年香港举办的东西方比较文学学术研讨会成果中选取了七篇代表性文章，以 *Chinese-Western Comparative Literature: Theory and Strategy* 为题集结出版，[19]并在其结语中附上那篇"中国学派"宣言文章以申明中国比较文学建立之必要。

学科开山之际，艰难险阻之巨难以想象，但从国际学者相关言论中可见西方对于中国比较文学学科的发展抱有的希望渺小。厄尔·迈纳（Earl Miner）

---

18 曹顺庆主编《比较文学概论》，高等教育出版社 2015 年版。

19 *Chinese-Western Comparative Literature：Theory & Strategy*，Chinese Univ Pr.1980-6

在 1987 年发表的 *Some Theoretical and Methodological Topics for Comparative Literature* 一文中谈到当时西方的比较文学鲜有学者试图将非西方材料纳入西方的比较文学研究中。（until recently there has been little effort to incorporate non-Western evidence into Western com- parative study.）1992 年，斯坦福大学教授 David Palumbo-Liu 直接以《话语的乌托邦：论中国比较文学的不可能性》为题（*The Utopias of Discourse: On the Impossibility of Chinese Comparative Literature*）直言中国比较文学本质上是一项"乌托邦"工程。（My main goal will be to show how and why the task of Chinese comparative literature, particularly of pre-modern literature, is essentially a *utopian* project.）这些对于中国比较文学的诘难与质疑，今美国加州大学圣地亚哥分校文学系主任张英进教授在其 1998 编著的 *China in a polycentric world: essays in Chinese comparative literature* 前言中也不得不承认中国比较文学研究在国际学术界中仍然处于边缘地位（The fact is, however, that Chinese comparative literature remained marginal in academia, even though it has developed closely with the rest of literary studies in the United Stated and even though China has gained increasing importance in the geopolitical world order over the past decades.）。[20]但张英进教授也展望了下一个千年中国比较文学研究的蓝景。

新的千年新的气象，"世界文学""全球化"等概念的冲击下，让西方学者开始注意到东方，注意到中国。如普渡大学教授斯蒂文·托托西（Tötösy de Zepetnek, Steven）1999 年发长文 *From Comparative Literature Today Toward Comparative Cultural Studies* 阐明比较文学研究更应该注重文化的全球性、多元性、平等性而杜绝等级划分的参与。托托西教授注意到了在法德美所谓传统的比较文学研究重镇之外，例如中国、日本、巴西、阿根廷、墨西哥、西班牙、葡萄牙、意大利、希腊等地区，比较文学学科得到了出乎意料的发展（emerging and developing strongly）。在这篇文章中，托托西教授列举了世界各地比较文学研究成果的著作，其中中国地区便是北京大学乐黛云先生出版的代表作品。托托西教授精通多国语言，研究视野也常具跨越性，新世纪以来也致力于以跨越性的视野关注世界各地比较文学研究的动向。[21]

---

20 Moran T . Yingjin Zhang, Ed. China in a Polycentric World: Essays in Chinese Comparative Literature[J].现代中文文学学报,2000,4(1):161-165.

21 Tötösy de Zepetnek, Steven. "From Comparative Literature Today Toward Comparative Cultural Studies." CLCWeb: Comparative Literature and Culture 1.3 (1999):

以上这些国际上不同学者的声音一则质疑中国比较文学建设的可能性，一则观望着这一学科在非西方国家的复兴样态。争议的声音不仅在国际学界，国内学界对于这一新兴学科的全局框架中涉及的理论、方法以及学科本身的立足点，例如前文所说的比较文学的定义，中国学派等等都处于持久论辩的漩涡。我们也通晓如果一直处于争议的漩涡中，便会被漩涡所吞噬，只有将论辩化为成果，才能转漩涡为涟漪，一圈一圈向外辐射，国际学人也在等待中国学者自己的声音。

上海交通大学王宁教授作为中国比较文学学者的国际发声者自 20 世纪末至今已撰文百余篇，他直言，全球化给西方学者带来了学科死亡论，但是中国比较文学必将在这全球化语境中更为兴盛，中国的比较文学学者一定会对国际文学研究做出更大的贡献。新世纪以来中国学者也不断地将自身的学科思考成果呈现在世界之前。2000 年，北京大学周小仪教授发文（*Comparative Literature in China*）[22]率先从学科史角度构建了中国比较文学在两个时期（20 世纪 20 年代至 50 年代，70 年代至 90 年代）的发展概貌，此文关于中国比较文学的复兴崛起是源自中国文学现代性的产生这一观点对美国芝加哥大学教授苏源熙（Haun Saussy）影响较深。苏源熙在 2006 年的专著 *Comparative Literature in an Age of Globalization* 中对于中国比较文学的讨论篇幅极少，其中心便是重申比较文学与中国文学现代性的联系。这篇文章也被哈佛大学教授大卫·达姆罗什（David Damrosch）收录于《普林斯顿比较文学资料手册》（*The Princeton Sourcebook in Comparative Literature*，2009[23]）。类似的学科史介绍在英语世界与法语世界都接续出现，以上大致反映了中国学者对于中国比较文学研究的大概描述在西学界的接受情况。学科史的构架对于国际学术对中国比较文学发展脉络的把握很有必要，但是在此基础上的学科理论实践才是关系于中国比较文学学科国际性发展的根本方向。

我在 20 世纪 80 年代以来 40 余年间便一直思考比较文学研究的理论构建问题，从以西方理论阐释中国文学而造成的中国文艺理论"失语症"思考

22 Zhou, Xiaoyi and Q.S. Tong, "Comparative Literature in China", Comparative Literature and Comparative Cultural Studies, ed., Totosy de Zepetnek, West Lafayette, Indiana: Purdue University Press, 2003, 268-283.

23 Damrosch, David (EDT)*The Princeton Sourcebook in Comparative Literature*: Princeton University Press

属于中国比较文学自身的学科方法论，从跨异质文化中产生的"文学误读""文化过滤""文学他国化"提出"比较文学变异学"理论。历经 10 年的不断思考，2013 年，我的英文著作：*The Variation Theory of Comparative Literature*（《比较文学变异学》），由全球著名的出版社之一斯普林格（Springer）出版社出版，并在美国纽约、英国伦敦、德国海德堡出版同时发行。*The Variation Theory of Comparative Literature*（《比较文学变异学》）系统地梳理了比较文学法国学派与美国学派研究范式的特点及局限，首次以全球通用的英语语言提出了中国比较文学学科理论新话语："比较文学变异学"。这一新概念、新范畴和新表述，引导国际学术界展开了对变异学的专刊研究（如普渡大学创办刊物《比较文学与文化》2017 年 19 期）和讨论。

欧洲科学院院士、西班牙圣地亚哥联合大学让·莫内讲席教授、比较文学系教授塞萨尔·多明戈斯教授（Cesar Dominguez），及美国科学院院士、芝加哥大学比较文学教授苏源熙（Haun Saussy）等学者合著的比较文学专著（Introducing Comparative literature: New Trends and Applications[24]）高度评价了比较文学变异学。苏源熙引用了《比较文学变异学》（英文版）中的部分内容，阐明比较文学变异学是十分重要的成果。与比较文学法国学派和美国学派形成对比，曹顺庆教授倡导第三阶段理论，即，新奇的、科学的中国学派的模式，以及具有中国学派本身的研究方法的理论创新与中国学派"（《比较文学变异学》（英文版）第 43 页）。通过对"中西文化异质性的"跨文明研究"，曹顺庆教授的看法会更进一步的发展与进步（《比较文学变异学》（英文版）第 43 页），这对于中国文学理论的转化和西方文学理论的意义具有十分重要的价值。（"Another important contribution in the direction of an imparative comparative literature-at least as procedure-is Cao Shunqing's 2013 *The Variation Theory of Comparative Literature*. In contrast to the "French School" and "American School" of comparative Literature, Cao advocates a "third-phrase theory", namely, "a novel and scientific mode of the Chinese school," a "theoretical innovation and systematization of the Chinese school by relying on our *own* methods" (*Variation Theory* 43; emphasis added). From this etic beginning, his proposal moves forward emically by developing a "cross-civilizaional study on the heterogeneity between

---

24 Cesar Dominguez,Haun Saussy,Dario Villanueva Introducing Comparative literature: New Trends and Applications，Routledge,2015

Chinese and Western culture" (43), which results in both the foreignization of Chinese literary theories and the Signification of Western literary theories.）

　　法国索邦大学（Sorbonne University）比较文学系主任伯纳德·弗朗科（Bernard Franco）教授在他出版的专著（《比较文学：历史、范畴与方法》）*La littératurecomparée: Histoire, domaines, méthodes* 中以专节引述变异学理论，他认为曹顺庆教授提出了区别于影响研究与平行研究的"第三条路"，即"变异理论"，这对应于观点的转变，从"跨文化研究"到"跨文明研究"。变异理论基于不同文明的文学体系相互碰撞为形式的交流过程中以产生新的文学元素，曹顺庆将其定义为"研究不同国家的文学现象所经历的变化"。因此曹顺庆教授提出的变异学理论概述了一个新的方向，并展示了比较文学在不同语言和文化领域之间建立多种可能的桥梁。（Il évoque l'hypothèse d'une troisième voie, la « théorie de la variation », qui correspond à un déplacement du point de vue, de celui des « études interculturelles » vers celui des « études transcivilisationnelles . » Cao Shunqing la définit comme « l'étude des variations subies par des phénomènes littéraires issus de différents pays, avec ou sans contact factuel, en même temps que l'étude comparative de l'hétérogénéité et de la variabilité de différentes expressions littéraires dans le même domaine ».Cette hypothèse esquisse une nouvelle orientation et montre la multiplicité des passerelles possibles que la littérature comparée établit entre domaines linguistiques et culturels différents.）[25]。

　　美国哈佛大学（Harvard University）厄内斯特·伯恩鲍姆讲席教授、比较文学教授大卫·达姆罗什（David Damrosch）对该专著尤为关注。他认为《比较文学变异学》（英文版）以中国视角呈现了比较文学学科话语的全球传播的有益尝试。曹顺庆教授对变异的关注提供了较为适用的视角，一方面超越了亨廷顿式简单的文化冲突模式，另一方面也跨越了同质性的普遍化。[26]国际学界对于变异学理论的关注已经逐渐从其创新性价值探讨延伸至文学研究，例如斯蒂文·托托西近日在 *Cultura* 发表的（Peripheralities: "Minor" Literatures, Women's Literature, and Adrienne Orosz de Csicser's Novels）一文中便成功地将变异学理论运用于阿德里安·奥罗兹的小说研究中。

25　Bernard Franco La littérature comparée: Histoire, domaines, méthodes，Armand Colin 2016.

26　David Damrosch Comparing the Literatures,Literary Studies in a Global Age,Princeton University Press,2020.

国际学界对于比较文学变异学的认可也证实了变异学作为一种普遍性理论提出的初衷，其合法性与适用性将在不同文化的学者实践中巩固、拓展与深化。它不仅仅是跨文明研究的方法，而是一种具有超越影响研究和平行研究、超越西方视角或东方视角的宏大视野、一种建立在文化异质性和变异性基础之上的融汇创生、一种追求世界文学和总体问题最终理想的哲学关怀。

以如此篇幅展现中国比较文学之况，是因为中国比较文学研究本就是在各种危机论、唱衰论的压力下，各种质疑论、概念论中艰难前行，不探源溯流难以体察今日中国比较文学研究成果之不易。文明的多样性发展离不开文明之间的交流互鉴。最具"跨文明"特征的比较文学学科更需要文明之间成果的共享、共识、共析与共赏，这是我们致力于比较文学研究领域的学术理想。

千里之行，不积跬步无以至，江海之阔，不积细流无以成！如此宏大的一套比较文学研究丛书得承花木兰总编辑杜洁祥先生之宏志，以及该公司同仁之辛劳，中国比较文学学者之鼎力相助，才可顺利集结出版，在此我要衷心向诸君表达感谢！中国比较文学研究仍有一条长远之途需跋涉，期以系列丛书一展全貌，愿读者诸君敬赐高见！

曹顺庆

二零二一年十月二十三日于成都锦丽园

序一　睿智的创译——读《李白望月的 150 种方式》有感

袁海旺

正如本书作者张智中教授所言，"西方人对于月亮，往往薄情寡义，而中国人的月亮情结，可谓月照流深"。本人曾经写过一首短文，不妨引来为张智中教授此番感慨作一个注脚：

> 在罗密欧和朱丽叶的眼里，她反复无常，她的暗影曾把奥塞罗逼得疯狂。马克·吐温用她像征人性晦暗和迷茫。唯有东方古国才赋予她光明的情感。神话里，后羿是嫦娥相隔浩渺的新郎，王建的秋思也是李白低头思念的故乡。张九龄从月上思远，张若虚在月下彷徨。"此事古难全，天地共婵娟！"苏东坡从月的阴晴圆缺感叹人间离合悲欢的苍凉。

中国人对月亮情有独钟，月亮在中国文化中承载着丰富的象征意义，嫦娥、吴刚等传说为其增添了神秘色彩，而圆月更是人们思乡之情的象征。今天，我们人手一台智能手机，通过互联网能够与远隔千山万水的亲朋好友联系。有意思的是，千午前，中国的诗人如李白、张九龄、王建、张若虚、苏东坡等，视月亮为人们超越时空进行心灵沟通的纽带，　如今日的人造卫星，让互联网成为可能。

写月亮的中国诗人也像夜空的繁星，数不胜数。而李白的这首《静夜思》，以其短小精悍、通俗易懂而著称。月光和思乡，成为《静夜思》中最为引人注目的意象，把身在异乡的古人对家乡的思念描绘得淋漓尽致，自然引起同时代和后人的共鸣。而且，其影响不仅跳过时间的长河，也跨越了地理空间，其魅力感染到诸如日本那样的邻国。翻译，特别是英译，更让这首小诗插上远飞的翅膀，在世界各个角落留下它令人遐思的回响。

有人说，诗歌是不可译的，在拼音文字的英文和表意文字的中文之间，更是如此。但这并不能阻挡睿智和勇敢的张智中教授大胆且有创意地去尝试，居然翻译出风格各异的一百六十种英译本（加上自序中的十种英译）。作者在对《月亮的重量》进行反思时，通过引用古代诗歌和现代诗作中的相关意象和诗句，展现了对诗歌创作的深刻理解和对文学传统的尊重。他将《静夜思》中的意象与其他诗作进行对比和联系，从而深化了对诗歌内涵的理解，体现了对诗歌语言和形式的敏锐洞察。作者将《静夜思》中的意象与李白其他作品及其他诗人的作品相对照，在其翻译中揭示了诗歌创作中的共通之处和个性特色。他对《静夜思》中每个意象生动和有创意的翻译，使读者更加深入地理解了诗歌所表达的情感和思想。此外，作者的一百六十种英译本，让读者不仅可以了解诗歌在不同语言和文化中的表达方式，还可以领略到诗歌翻译的艺术魅力和难度。

作者张智中教授通过尝试各种风格的翻译，为深入剖析《静夜思》这首诗歌的内涵和形式，进而丰富对诗歌的理解和欣赏做出了杰出的贡献。他的贡献还不止于此，其对《静夜思》的翻译、分析和研究，不仅为读者提供了一种全新的阅读视角，也为诗歌研究和翻译实践提供了有益的参考和启示。

袁海旺

美国肯塔基大学荣休教授、作者、译者

南开大学外国语学院中华诗词外译中心顾问

2024 年 2 月 7 日

美国肯塔基州宝灵格林市

序二　奇文共欣赏——《李白望月的 150 种方式》代序

冯全功

　　如果要问中国最著名的古代诗人是谁，相信很多人会说是李白；如果要问李白的哪首诗最为有名，相信很多人会说是《静夜思》。李白的《静夜思》短短二十个字，含蕴丰富，韵味悠长，冲击着历代读者的心灵，尤其是漂泊他乡的游子。

　　这首诗中的"明月"最为神奇，诗人举头看到了明月，低头便想起了故乡，毕竟月是故乡的明，毕竟明月可以照诗人还乡。然而，千里共婵娟，明月何曾是两乡……明月承载着诗人的绵绵乡愁，承载着诗人的殷殷期盼，承载着诗人的小小慰藉。

　　还清晰地记得孩子津津牙牙学语之时，经常抱着他，给他朗诵李白的《静夜思》，也算是教他学说话吧，于是《静夜思》便成了孩子会背的第一首诗，当时也就一岁多点而已。目前津津已经上小学二年级，前不久他们的语文卷子上有这么一道题："你学过哪些描写月亮的古诗句？"他一口气写了十句，其中第一句便是李白的"床前明月光，疑是地上霜。"其他还有"海上生明月，大涯共此时"；"举杯邀明月，对影成三人"；"深林人不知，明月来相照"；"明月别枝惊鹊，清风半夜鸣蝉"；"沧海月明珠有泪，蓝田日暖玉生烟"；"刚被太阳收拾去，又教明月送将来"等。明月就这样变成了中华儿女共同的文化记忆，或寄托乡思之情，或传递恋爱之情，或表达隐逸之情，或抒发恬淡之情，不一而足。

　　中国古代诗人大多都有较强的明月情结，李白无疑是最典型的代表。相传李白在安徽当涂的江上饮酒，喝醉了就跳入江水中捉那水中的月亮，从此便与明月"万古同辉"了。李白的明月，拨动着历代文人的心弦，尤其是他的《静夜思》，诗中的明月蕴含着浓郁的乡愁，成为望月思乡的经典之作。《静夜思》广被吟诵，代代如此，多是由于那轮明月的魅力吧。

　　南开大学张智中教授是一位卓有成就的翻译家，已翻译出版了大量中国古典诗词。他最喜欢的古诗词莫过于李白的《静夜思》。近些年，通过阅读大量英文，借鉴英文中相关优美地道的表达，同时充分发挥自己的想象力，调动自己的创造性，张智中教授对《静夜思》的翻译已经有了一百多个版本。他把这些英译版本汇集起来，再加上其他相关内容，如所读到的英文句子、所译成的英诗回译、译者本人对其译文的剖析与翻译感悟等，于是便有了这本《李白望月的 150 种方式》。作者拟定的标题很有趣，"李白望月"化自诗中的"举头望明月"，代表原诗《静夜思》，"150 种方式"也就是自己的 150 种不同的翻译，或措辞不同，或组句不同，或韵律不同，或视角不同，或方法不同，或繁简不同……李白的《静夜思》在英语世界应该也有几百个版本，但凭一己之力独自翻译一百多个版本的绝对只此一家。

　　张智中教授为什么会翻译如此多的《静夜思》版本呢？恐怕只能用痴迷二字来回答，痴迷于李白的《静夜思》，痴迷于古典诗词的翻译，痴迷于英文的表达力，痴迷于语言本身的魅力。2018 年，他曾在"青年翻译学者论坛"微信群里说，"诗歌就是一种感悟，译诗也是一种感悟"——"感悟出真知！"李白《静夜思》的众多翻译就是他"感悟"出来的，不同的时期有不同的感悟，不同的感悟造就了不同的版本。感悟与想象是分不开的，感悟是"神与物游"的结果，"我才之多少，将与风云而并驱矣"。张智中教授颇有诗才，在翻译《静夜思》时想象丰富，感悟深刻，再加上善于借鉴英文中的相关表达，催发出了一首又一首的英译版本。这是情不自禁的翻译冲动，是痴迷于诗歌与诗歌翻译之使然。

　　能够产生如此多的《静夜思》英译版本，也得益于张智中教授灵活变通的翻译观或译诗观，从而打破严格忠实观的束缚，为自己的创造性发挥提供了广阔的空间。他有时把自己的译诗观命名为"解构主义翻译观"，认为其最大优点便是能够充分发挥译者的想象力与创造力。这里的"解构"应该是指解语言表层之构，破僵硬忠实之念，通过增删切合等各种变通译法，把原诗的意旨与意境传达出来。从这点而言，张智中教授的译诗观也不妨视为是一种深层的忠实、审美的忠实、整体的忠实。《静夜思》原文只有 20 个汉字，他的译文有与原文同样简洁的，如"望月之4"，英译才13个单词；也有非常繁复的，如"望月之18"，英译多达165个单词，是前者的十多倍。就回译而言，在"望月之41"的"译人语"中，作者说："《静夜思》是五言绝句，才20个汉字，译文却203个字，正好十倍。似乎过分，但是，仔细想来，添加的，都是李白不曾道出的细节。"增译是作者的常用译法，尤其是增添相关话语，不失为其"解构"译法的主要手段，旨在烘托原诗的意境。译者还会反复增添一些意象，如dream, eyes, heart, window, childhood等，与原诗中的固有意象相得益彰。译者有时不惜整句整句地增添相关话语来烘托原诗的意境，如"望月之22"中的"I seem to catch glimpses of the mellow light of my childhood moon, suggestive of my hometown, my villagers, my neighbors, my sisters and brothers, and my parents...."；"望月之45"中的"My thoughts are far away, over rills after rills and across hills upon hills, to the little corner of the earth where my childhood has been lived."；"望月之84"中的"Homesickness is always annexed to the moon, and the moon is his who watches it."等等。

读英文，译古诗，是张智中教授一贯秉承的翻译理念，也就是通过大量的英文阅读来提高自己的英语表达能力，把相关英语表达巧妙地融入到自己的译文之中，化为自己译文的血肉，使之更具可读性与艺术感染力。这种理念在该著中表现得淋漓尽致，尤其是"读英文"与"译人语"部分，作者对自己是如何借鉴相关英文表达的，也都有或详或略的介绍。借鉴地道的英语表达，再加上译者的创造性运用，使其译文变得颇有灵气，韵味十足。不管是原创英语还是翻译英语，诗歌语言还是小说语言，只要是地道的、优美的、切合具体语境的，都可以拿来所用。带着翻译意识去学习英语，这是张智中教授汉诗英译的不二法门。

张智中教授是一位"向诗而生"的译者。他的译文很耐读，很多表达也颇有趣味，如"望月之53"中的"We beam at each other, the moon and me..."；"望月之85"中的"The moon is long, as long as homesickness."；"望月之146"中的"...dreams about my native land which, out of sight for dozens of years, is never out of mind."等。此类佳例，不胜枚举。此外，他还为150种《静夜思》的英译拟定了150个不同的英语标题，回译成现代汉语也不拘格套，韵味悠长，如把"望月之4"的标题"Moonward & Homeward"译为"向月·向家"；把"望月之131"的标题"The Moon as a Spellbinder"译为"月亮醉

我";把"望月之 113"的标题"The Moon as an Inducer of Nostalgia"译为"乡愁：都是月亮惹的祸";把"望月之 101"的标题"For Whom the Moon Rises?"译为"明月为谁而升？"等。最后一个英译标题及其回译，明显套用了海明威的小说 For Whom the Bell Tolls 及其对应汉译《丧钟为谁而鸣》。诸如此类的引用或化用在该著中还有很多，也为译诗平添了一抹亮色。

苏东坡曾说，"诗以奇趣为宗，反常合道为趣"。张智中教授的《李白望月的 150 种方式》是一部充满"奇趣"的书，不管是英译还是回译，抑或译人语，莫不如此。

让我们一块遨游其中，共赏书中的奇趣吧！

冯全功

2024 年 2 月 6 日

浙江大学紫金西苑

序三 不堪盈手赠——《静夜思》英译杂感

张智中

泱泱诗国，诗海浩瀚。

纵横诗史，若选出一首最受欢迎的诗作，我想，非李白之《静夜思》莫属的吧：

> 床前明月光，疑是地上霜。举头望明月，低头思故乡。

不仅国内，邻国日本，亦是如此。"日本教科书中的中国汉诗大多数是唐诗，部分先秦、魏晋南北朝、宋代、明代的作品。从所选诗人来看，李白、杜甫、白居易出现的频率最高。从选用次数来看，李白《静夜思》居首位。"[1]

"本诗是在寂静夜晚思念家乡的经典诗作。……这首诗寥寥数语便将主题表现得淋漓尽致，如清水芙蓉，不带半点修饰，一切均从心底自然流出，宛如天籁，以致千百年来脍炙人口，流传不衰！"[2]

近日网络上读到《人民日报》点评："短短四句诗，写得清新朴素。它的构思是细致而深曲的，但却又是脱口吟成、浑然无迹的。"

诗中两个意象：月光，冷霜。

"从'光'到'霜'，从视觉影像到有手感的物质，其间转化，似乎含有创世密码，若无这两个诗眼，诗便俗，有了就神。"[3]

《静夜思》中的"床前"和"地上"，乃是异乡的"床前"和"地上"。

---

1 李均洋，后记［A］，李均洋，（日）佐藤利行，荣喜朝主编，风月同天：日本人眼中最美中国古诗 100 首［C］，北京：人民文学出版社，2020：232。

2 陈书良，诗词之美［M］，北京：作家出版社，2016：55。

3 刘刚，莫奈的诗囊［M］，北京：商务印书馆，2016：105。

"他乡没有烈酒，没有问候。"（《九月九的酒》陈树 作词）因此，"冷霜"总是难免的；因此，思乡也是难免的。《静夜思》中的核心意象，乃是月亮；月亮与乡愁，随之而成为黏连之物。

在现存李白的千首诗作中，《静夜思》流传最广，而《静夜思》的核心意象，乃是月亮。"中国人之所以喜欢月亮，是因为月亮上面有嫦娥与吴刚。'嫦娥应悔偷灵药，碧海青天夜夜心'——这是寂寞的嫦娥；'吴刚捧出桂花酒'——这是热情的吴刚。一轮圆月，在寄托了我们美好想象的同时也开拓了我们的情感世界。"[4]

另外，"在中国文化里，月亮代表着超凡脱俗。"[5]因此，凡中国人，没有不喜欢月亮的。中国还有一个重要的节日：中秋节。中秋节，其实也叫月亮节。这天，人们不仅赏月，还要吃月亮形状的月饼。对于月亮的渴望，于此可见。

中国文学史上关于月亮的古诗，太多了，可谓卷帙浩繁、盈千累万，若恒河沙数。聊举数例：

中秋对月
唐·曹松

无云世界秋三五，共看蟾盘上海涯。直到天头天尽处，不曾私照一人家。

此乃移情入诗之月。

中秋月
宋·苏轼

暮云收尽溢清寒，银汉无声转玉盘。此生此夜不长好，明月明年何处看？

此乃多情伤感之月。

池州翠微亭
宋·岳飞

经年尘土满征衣，特特寻芳上翠微。好水好山看不足，马蹄催趁月明归。

4 单世联，知识人的关怀与压力［M］，北京：商务印书馆，2016：153。
5 韩希明，诗与童真——给孩子的古代童诗经典［M］，成都：四川辞书出版社，2019：152。

此乃思乡照明之月。

月夜

唐·杜甫

今夜鄜州月，闺中只独看。遥怜小儿女，未解忆长安。香雾云鬟湿，清辉玉臂寒。何时倚虚幌，双照泪痕干。

此乃思念观望之月。

情

唐·吴融

依依脉脉两如何，细似轻丝渺似波。月不长圆花易落，一生惆怅为伊多。

此乃惆怅落寞之月。

中秋月

唐·李峤

圆魄上寒空，皆言四海同。安知千里外，不有雨兼风。

此乃哲思深情之月。

山居秋暝

唐·王维

空山新雨后，天气晚来秋。明月松间照，清泉石上流。竹喧归浣女，莲动下渔舟。随意春芳歇，王孙自可留。

此乃幽雅清新之月。

月夜

唐·华山老人

涧水泠泠声不绝，溪流茫茫野花发。自去自来人不知，归时常对空山月。

此乃空灵缥缈之月。

牧童

唐·吕严

草铺横野六七里，笛弄晚风三四声。归来饭饱黄昏后，不脱蓑衣卧月明。

此乃温馨可人之月。

忆扬州

唐 · 徐凝

萧娘脸下难胜泪，桃叶眉头易得愁。天下三分明月夜，二分无赖是扬州。

此乃月光皎皎之月。

送柴侍御

唐 · 王昌龄

沅水通波接武冈，送君不觉有离伤。青山一道同云雨，明月何曾是两乡。

此乃天涯海角之月。

碛中作

唐 · 岑参

走马西来欲到天，辞家见月两回圆。今夜未知何处宿，平沙莽莽绝人烟。

此乃计时算日之月。

从军北征

唐 · 李益

天山雪后海风寒，横笛偏吹行路难。碛里征人三十万，一时回首月中看。

此乃服役士兵之月。

忆东山二首（一）

唐 · 李白

不向东山久，蔷薇几度花。白云还自散，明月落谁家。

此乃悠闲浪漫之月。

芦花

唐 · 雍裕之

夹岸复连沙，枝枝摇浪花。月明浑似雪，无处认渔家。

此乃朦胧模糊之月。

马诗（其五）

唐 · 李贺

大漠沙如雪，燕山月似钩。何当金络脑，快走踏清秋。

此乃冷漠淡然之月。

明月夜留别

唐·李冶

离人无语月无声，明月有光人有情。别后相思人似月，云间水上到层城。

此乃思念入骨之月。

寄人

唐·张泌

别梦依依到谢家，小廊回合曲阑斜。多情只有春庭月，犹为离人照落花。

此乃魂牵梦萦之月。

待山月

唐·皎然

夜夜忆故人，长教山月待。今宵故人至，山月知何在。

此乃故人似来之月。

咏月

唐·李建枢

昨夜圆非今夜圆，却疑圆处减婵娟。一年十二度圆缺，能得几多时少年？

此乃阴晴圆缺之月。

望月怀远

唐·张九龄

海上生明月，天涯共此时。情人怨遥夜，竟夕起相思。灭烛怜光满，披衣觉露滋。不堪盈手赠，还寝梦佳期。

此乃情人遥思之月。

月下独酌

唐·李白

花间一壶酒，独酌无相亲。举杯邀明月，对影成三人。月既不解饮，影徒随我身。暂伴月将影，行乐须及春。我歌月徘徊，我舞影零乱。醒时同交欢，醉后各分散。永结无情游，相期邈云汉。

此乃醉酒寻欢之月。

出塞

唐·王昌龄

秦时明月汉时关，万里长征人未还。但使龙城飞将在，不教胡马度阴山。

此乃马革裹尸之月。

盆池

唐·杜牧

凿破苍苔地，偷他一片天。白云生镜里，明月落阶前。

此乃天光云影之月。

有寄

唐·杜牧

云阔烟深树，江澄水浴秋。美人何处在？明月万山头。

此乃明月万山之月。

江楼闻砧

唐·白居易

江人授衣晚，十月始闻砧。一夕高楼月，万里故园心。

此乃登高伤感之月。

上元夜六首（一）

唐·崔液

玉漏铜壶且莫催，铁关金锁彻明开。谁家见月能闲坐，何处闻灯不看来。

此乃节日狂欢之月。

江楼感旧

唐·赵嘏

独上江楼思渺然，月光如水水如天。同来望月人何处？风景依稀似去年。

此乃柔情似水之月。

子夜吴歌

唐·李白

长安一片月，万户捣衣声。秋风吹不尽，总是玉关情。何日平胡虏，良人罢远征。

此乃秋夜劳作之月。

竹里馆

唐·王维

独坐幽篁里，弹琴复长啸。深林人不知，明月来相照。

此乃出世旷达之月。

拜新月

唐·李端

开帘见新月，即便下阶拜。细语人不闻，北风吹罗带。

幼女词

唐·施肩吾

幼女才六岁，未知巧与拙。向夜在堂前，学人拜新月。

此二诗者，乃崇敬跪拜之月。这在英语世界里，该是不可理解的吧。

　　最近几天，又读到清人徐韦的一首绝句：

对月

清·徐韦

愁心化为水，荡漾明月光。将心寄明月，堕地忽成霜。[6]

既"光"且"霜"，与李白之《静夜思》，甚相仿佛，可谓新版的静夜之月。

　　近人李叔同也写过一首题为《月》的诗作：

月

李叔同

仰碧空明月，朗月悬太清。瞰下界扰扰，尘欲迷中道！惟愿灵
光普万方，荡涤垢滓扬芬芳。虚渺无极，圣洁神秘，灵光常仰望！

仰碧空明月，朗月悬太清。瞰下界暗暗，世路多愁叹！惟愿灵
光普万方，拔除痛苦散清凉。虚渺无极，圣洁神秘，灵光常仰望！

此乃如佛出尘之月。

　　又，近日英译周瑟瑟先生的诗集《鹧鸪与木梯》，其中一首最为喜欢：

月亮的重量

大海承受月亮的重量

压抑的鲸鱼奋起打破月亮的平静

---

6 陈友琴，千首清人绝句校注［Z］，杭州：浙江古籍出版社，2019：209。

　　　　鲸鱼为什么哭泣？在月圆之夜
　　　　大海上的光辉属于逝去的亲人
　　　　月亮顺道照亮了人间
　　　　与我们共享千年的清辉

　　首行"大海承受月亮的重量"，令人想起张九龄《望月怀远》中的"海上生明月，天涯共此时"，以及张若虚《春江花月夜》中的"滟滟随波千万里，何处春江无月明"。月照江海——大海不可承受月亮之重。

　　第二行"压抑的鲸鱼奋起打破月亮的平静"，令人想起李商隐《锦瑟》中的"沧海月明珠有泪"，含有鲛人泣珠的典故：鲛人的泪水，化作了一粒粒珍珠；想起悲痛伤心的往事，心情沉重，仿佛沧海明月下的珠儿，颗颗都带着眼泪。"鲸鱼"，似通鲛人；泣珠流泪，月之平静不复。

　　接着，诗人发问："鲸鱼为什么哭泣？"，答曰："在月圆之夜/大海上的光辉属于逝去的亲人"。苏轼《江城子》云："料得年年肠断处，明月夜，短松冈。"于是，明月与对已故亲人的思念，关系愈加密切了。

　　第五行："月亮顺道照亮了人间"，想起王建《十五夜望月寄杜郎中》中的诗句："今夜月明人尽望，不知秋思落谁家？"这里的秋思，乃是哀思。

　　最后一行："与我们共享千年的清辉"，令人诗思逸飞，浮想联翩：从《诗经·月出》中的"月出皎兮，佼人僚兮"，到苏轼《水调歌头》中的"明月几时有？把酒问青天"，到张若虚《春江花月夜》中的"江畔何人初见月？江月何年初照人？"再到李白《古朗月行》中的"小时不识月，呼作白玉盘"，及其《把酒问月》中的"今人不见古时月，今月曾经照古人。"凡此种种，都加大了《月亮的重量》，成为大海不堪承受之重。

　　没有古诗的积淀，写不出这样的诗作；没有古诗的底子，读不懂这样的诗作。含标题计 73 字的短诗《月亮的重量》，当为新诗之杰作。

　　总之，中国人的内心，都有着一种所谓的月亮情结。月照人间，向来久远。古代中国乃农业社会，在无电缺油的古代，月亮是人们的夜晚之灯。在汉语中，月亮有多种叫法或"昵称"："玉壶"、"冰轮"、"蟾蜍"、"宝鉴"、"顾菟"、"圆魄"、"宵魄"、"半弓"、"婵娟"、"玉兔"、"月轮"、"桂魄"、"桂蟾"、"嫦娥"、"冰兔"、"夜明"、"蟾宫"、"太阴"、"桂月"、"桂兔"等，足见中国人对月亮的喜爱；再加上关于月亮的神话传说：月宫、婵娟、吴刚、桂树……，中国人对于月亮，可谓一往而情深。

因此，中国诗人，尤其是古代诗人，几乎没有不写月亮的。而写月亮之最者，恐怕还是《静夜思》的作者李白，有人统计，李白写月亮的诗作多达 400 多首，占其诗作的三分之一。而且，李白捞月而死的浪漫传说，连美国诗人庞德都知道，并写之入诗：

Epitaphs	**墓志铭**
Fu I	傅奕
Fu I loved the high cloud and the hill,	傅奕，
Alas, he died of alcohol.	青山白云人也，
	因酒醉死，
Li Po	呜呼哀哉。
And Li Po also died drunk.	李白
He tried to embrace a moon	李白，
In the Yellow River.	亦因酒而亡，
	为圆揽月梦，
	捐躯黄河中。
	（荣立宇　译）[7]

"翻译说明"如下：

"两篇墓志铭乃庞德为中国古代两位饮酒而亡的诗人所做，所谓'怅惘千秋一洒泪，萧条异代不同时'。描述见解，感慨颇多。为了凸显墓志铭这种文体的庄重，译诗使用了较为文雅的措辞和句式。如'……（者），……也''呜呼哀哉'等。为李白所作的最后两行凑成五言一联，则是为了彰显李白的诗人身份。"[8]

相较而言，西方的月亮，内涵就单薄多了。就月亮的称谓而言，汉语如上诸多，而英文却只一个 moon，英文诗篇中写到月亮的，本为少数，即便写到，也往往疯狂或病态。例如爱尔兰著名诗人叶芝的这首及其汉译：

7　（美）埃兹拉·庞德 著；王宏印，杨森，荣立宇选译，庞德诗歌精译：英汉对照 [Z]，天津：南开大学出版社，2022：322-323。

8　（美）埃兹拉·庞德 著；王宏印，杨森，荣立宇选译，庞德诗歌精译：英汉对照 [Z]，天津：南开大学出版社，2022：322-324。

The Crazy Moon	疯月亮
Crazed through much child-bearing	因为生子过多而发疯，
The moon is staggering in the sky;	月亮在天空蹒跚而行；
Moon-struck by the despairing	她那游荡的眼神一瞥，
Glances of her wandering eye	绝望的一瞥错乱了神经，
We grope, and grope in vain,	我们摸索，徒然地摸索，
For children born of her pain.	她的阵痛诞生了子女多多。
Children dazed or dead!	子女们有的目眩，有的死亡！
When she in all her virginal pride	当年的她自有童贞的傲狂，
First trod on the mountain's head	第一次走上山头翩翩起舞，
What stir ran through the countryside	把骚乱传遍了广大的农乡，
Where every foot obeyed her glance!	她的眼神支配着每一个脚步！
What manhood led the dance!	什么样的男子在领头起舞！
Fly-catchers of the moon,	月光洒落犹如捕蝇草，
Our hands are blenched, our fingers seem	我们的双手收缩，十指根根
But slender needles of bone;	缩变成根根细细的骨针；
Blenched by that malicious dream	被那邪恶的梦幻熏染得发白，
They are spread wide that each	我们十指开张伸向四方，
May rend what comes in reach.	指到哪里哪里就被刺伤。
	（王宏印 译）[9]

"月亮在不同的文化中，意象和涵义迥异，中国文化中的圆满、团圆荡然无存，变为丑陋疯狂的女人形象，这是英文诗歌里常见形象，例如在雪莱的诗中就有相似的类比。但叶芝的应用更加具有魔幻色彩，所以要译出效果来。"[10]

总之，西方人对于月亮，往往薄情寡义，而中国人的月亮情结，可谓月照流深。

让我们再回到《静夜思》："这首诗在内容上单纯而又丰富，在艺术上明了

9 （爱尔兰）威廉·叶芝著；王宏印，苏易安选译，叶芝诗歌精译：英汉对照 [Z]，天津：南开大学出版社，2022：298-299。

10 （爱尔兰）威廉·叶芝著；王宏印，苏易安选译，叶芝诗歌精译：英汉对照 [Z]，天津：南开大学出版社，2022：300。

而又含蓄，在语言上更是天然独至。"[11]因此，《静夜思》的翻译，是高难度的。在论及《静夜思》的英译之前，我们先来看两首今译：

床前一片明月光， 怀疑地上生秋霜。 抬头遥望天上月， 低头思念我故乡。[12]	望床前皎洁的月光， 原以为是地上的寒霜。 抬起头来才看到天上明月， 却又低下头去想着故乡。[13]

原诗的尾韵："光"、"霜"、"乡"，两种今译，也是"光"、"霜"、"乡"，抄袭原诗的尾韵，不做任何改变。语言上，在原诗五言的基础上，变成七言或杂言，稍微拉长句子，填充一些累词赘语，便算完成了诗歌翻译的任务。这种翻译，只是机械的"字译"，不是诗意的翻译。如此拘泥的译文，胶柱而鼓瑟，绝非诗歌译者的本色。

来看两种中国译者的英译：

Thoughts on a Quiet Night	**Homesickness in a Quiet, Moonlit Night**
In front of my bed there's a stream of moonlight, Which is suspected by me to be autumn frost on the ground. Raising my head I gaze at the moon bright, Bowing my head by homesickness my thought is bound.[14]	What bright moonbeams are beside my bed in room! Could on the ground there be the frost so soon? Lifting my head, I see a big, full moon, Only to bend to think of my sweet home.[15]

两个译文都是格律体，分别押交叉韵 abab 和抱韵 abba；前者语言上啰里啰嗦，后者亦语言生硬，如 in room，there be the frost so soon，to bend 等。两种译文，若回译成汉语，则与上引两种"今译"差别不大。再看两种英美汉学家的英译：

11 戴建业，激发孩子想象力的古诗 100 首 [M]，上海：复旦大学出版社，2021：178。
12 郑竹青，周双利，中国历代诗歌通典 [C]，北京：解放军出版社，1999：1393。
13 章培恒，李白集 [C]，南京：凤凰出版社，2020：251。
14 王福林，唐诗三百首详注·英译·浅析：普及读本 [Z]，南京：东南大学出版社，2015：379。
15 王大濂，英译唐诗绝句百首 [Z]，天津：百花文艺出版社，1997：53。

In the Quiet Night	Thoughts on a Quiet Night
So bright a gleam on the foot of my bed —	Beside my bed, the bright moon lit the floor;
Could there have been a frost already?	waking, at first I thought it was the frost.
Lifting myself to look, I found that it was moonlight.	I looked up to see the bright moon shining,
Sinking back again, I thought suddenly of home.	then bowed my head to think of home again.
(Witter Bynner & Kiang Kang-hu 译)[16]	（Geoffrey R. Waters 译）[17]

　　都是自由体译诗。后者首行 the bright moon lit the floor（明月点亮了地板），似有诗意，其余皆平淡之措词用语，看不出多少高明之处。"一个真正优秀的译者不是'翻译机器'，他的译文必得带着其独具的理解力和创造力，带着他自己脉搏的跳动和生命印记，带着原著与译文之间那种'必要的张力'。"[18] 这就说到了点子上。胶柱鼓瑟的译文，不可能出彩；唯译者独具理解力和创造力，译文才能取得较好的审美效果。

　　《静夜思》的英译，尤其如此。"中国文学中锤炼的，西文最难翻译；但弹性的、悠扬的，可以翻。"[19] 显然，《静夜思》是"锤炼的"，也因其平易近人而难于翻译。《静夜思》貌似单纯，内容却极大地丰富。有一千个读者，便有一千个《静夜思》的解读，虽然大体方向一致，在细节的联想上，却各呈其异。其实，即便是同一个读者，在不同的时空，在不同的人生阶段，也会想起《静夜思》，而内心涌起不同的波澜，有着稍微不同的人生感悟。这，就是《静夜思》可以一直翻译下去的原因。

　　李白望月的 150 种方式，即是对《静夜思》150 种不同的英译和阐释。有直译者，有意译者；有格律者，有自由者；有精短者，有繁冗者；有拘泥者，

16 Witter Bynner & Kiang Kang-hu. The Jade Mountain, a Chinese Anthology: Being Three Hundred Poems of the T'ang Dynasty 618-906[Z]. New York: Alfred A. Knopf, Inc., 1929: 53.
17 Geoffrey R. Waters, Michael Farman & David Lunde. Three Hundred Tang Poems[Z]. Buffalo, New York: White Pine Press, 2011: 183.
18 王家新，在一颗名叫哈姆雷特的星下 [M]，北京：中国人民大学出版社，2012：314。
19 顾随讲、刘在昭笔记、顾之京、高献红整理，中国经典原境界 [M]，北京：北京大学出版社，2016：85。

有开放者；有忠实者，有解构者……，都是对《静夜思》的不同阐释。这些译文的完成，大概持续了三、四年，而且，还在翻译中。近日，又完成了《静夜思》的10种英译，兹录于此。

英文阅读：

He painted by **stilling** his mind, in a process both painful and therapeutic.	他静下心来作画，这是痛苦和治愈的过程。
Caroline **felt suddenly very happy**.	卡罗琳突然感到非常高兴。
"Are you **feeling nostalgic**?" "**Emotional**, maybe."	"你在怀旧吗？" "可能是情绪化吧。"
She felt **a pang of longing for** spotless suburbia.	她对一尘不染的郊区感到一阵渴望。
A pang of pain had shot through his body.	他感到全身一阵剧痛。

英译一：

Still Night Thoughts

A shaft of light into the room

— a frosty floor. Upward

looking, to find a bright moon

stilling everything, and I feel

suddenly very emotional, or

nostalgic; a pang of longing

for home shoots through

my body, as the moonlight

shoots through the window.

英文阅读：

Jill crossed her legs and rested her chin on one fist, as if lost in **deep thought**.	吉尔两腿交叉，下巴抵在拳头上，似乎陷入了沉思。
Moonlight was **silvering** the countryside.	月光下的乡村泛着银光。
She **lowered her head in thought**.	她低下头沉思。

英译二：

Deep Night, Deep Thought

In front of my bed
the moon is bright,
suggestive of frost
silvering the ground.
I lift my gaze toward
the moon, before lowering
my head in thought.

英文阅读：

Contained within the apparent peacefulness of the scene is **a lurking** threat.	在这个看起来和谐安详的画面中，却隐含着危险。
The unearthly stillness of rural twilight came stealthily down about her.	乡间暮色神秘的寂静，悄悄来到她身边。
She looked down the road for him, **the pain in her heart swelling up** again.	她沿大路看去，心底的疼痛又一次弥漫开来。

英译三：

A Lurking Homesickness

A film of frost on the ground?
I lift my head to trace its source
— a bright moon without
the window, and the unearthly
stillness of moonlight is coming
stealthily down about me. Then
I lower my head in thought, and
the pain in my heart, a lurking
homesickness, is swelling up.

英文阅读：

Desperately she longed for her mother's return from the Slatterys', for, without her, she **felt lost and alone**.	她急切渴望妈妈快点儿从斯兰特瑞家回来，没有她，她觉得失落和孤独。

It was a prim, virginal little room and **it lay still** and warm **in the slanting rays of the four-o'clock sun**.	这是一间整洁的小闺房, 安静而温暖地沐浴在下午四点斜照的阳光里。

英译四:

Desperate Longing for Home

At the sight of the silver-

frosted floor, I find my

little room is lying still

in the slanting rays of

the midnight bright moon

and, feeling lost and alone

for so many years, I

desperately long for home.

英文阅读:

The bellow of aligators broke **the night stillness**.	鳄鱼的吼声打破夜的寂静。
The floors were glistening and bare except for a few bright rag rugs.	除了几块地毯外, 光滑的地板上空空荡荡。
She **dragged her eyes away from** him without smiling back.	她没有回笑, 把目光从他身上收了回来。
Despite her and the pain for unshed tears, **a deep sense of quiet and peace fell upon** Scarlett as it always did at his hour.	尽管悲痛欲绝, 泪水忍住才没流下来, 一种深深的宁静平和感还是包围了斯卡特里, 在这个时刻, 她总会这样。
She **dismissed the thought**.	她把这所有的一切念头都抛开了。

英译五:

Homesick Through the Night Stillness

The floor is glistening

and bare except for

a few patches of frosty
light, and I drag my eyes
away from the floor,
toward a bright moon
outside the window,
a deep sense of quiet
and peace falling upon
me. I cannot dismiss
the thought of home.

英文阅读：

Coolness **was beginning to come back to her** and **her mind was collecting itself**.	她渐渐恢复了冷静，思维也开始集中了。
Lying in the bed with moonlight streaming dimly **over her**, she pictured the whole scence in her mind.	躺在床上，月光朦胧地泻在她身上，她在脑海里刻画了整个画面。
"They were divine," she sighs, **dreamily**.	"他们是神圣的，"她神情恍惚地叹了口气。

英译六：

Homesickness: My Mind Is Collecting Itself

Lying in the bed with
moonlight streaming
silverily over me, I find
the floor dreamily frosty
from a bright moon
without the window.
Homesickness is beginning
to come back to me, and
my mind is collecting
itself.

英文阅读：

The quiet of moonlight nights and the serene charm of the old house.	万籁无声的月夜和那幢古老的住宅宁静的美。
A frost lay over all her emotions and she thought that she would never feel anything warmly again.	一层雾笼罩在她全部的感情之上，她想她再也不会感觉到什么事情了。

英译七：

The Quiet of Moonlight Night

The quiet of moonlight

night and the serene

charm of my little house,

I sense it as I catch

a glimpse of the frosty

floor before my bed.

A frost lies over

all my emotions and

I think that I would never

feel anything warmly again

— except my family,

my home.

英文阅读：

My longing to return to true country life has been answered, complete with a beautiful waterhole.	我渴望回归真正乡村生活的愿望得以实现，还有一个漂亮的水池——真是锦上添花。
I could elicit no response from him.	我从他那里套不出任何反应。

英译八：

My Longing to Return Home

Light?

frost?

— on the floor of my bedroom.

upward looking:

shining moon-

light in the dead of night

elicits my longing

to return

home

英文阅读：

The sight of a tailor-shop **gave me a sharp longing to** shed my rags, and to clothe myself decently once more.	当我看到一家裁缝店时，心里有股强烈的渴望，想脱掉这身破衣服，重新换上体面的服装。
I stopped, of course, and **fastened my desiring eye on** that muddy treasure.	我当然停了下来，一双渴望的眼睛紧紧地盯着那个沾满烂泥的宝贝。
She **fell into a train of melancholy thoughts**.	她陷进了一种连续不绝的忧郁思想里。

英译九：

Still Night, Still Thoughts

The sigh of a bright moon

before my bed, suggestive

of hoarfrost on the ground,

gives me a sharp longing

to be back home.

I fasten my desiring eye

on the moon,

before falling

into a train of

melancholy

thoughts.

英文阅读：

Sunlight **washed over his face**.	阳光照在他脸上。
I **squinted against** the blinding white.	雪花反射出白晃晃的光芒，照得我睁不开眼。

I **tried to peel my gaze from** our rooftop.	我试图让眼光离开我们家的屋顶。
Wide reading will **increase** your vocabulary.	博览群书会增加你的词汇量。
However Zambrotta's wife, Valentina, is said to have become **increasingly homesick** and is desperate to move back to Italy as soon as possible.	但是，赞布罗塔的妻子瓦伦蒂娜的思乡情绪愈加浓烈，她希望能尽快回到意大利生活。
The silly dream had **lifted** some of my anxiety.	那个愚蠢的梦缓解了我的焦虑。

英译十：

Still Night Thoughts

The moonlight washes

over my face, against

which I squint —

to find hoarfrost

on the ground?

From the moon I

try to peel my gaze,

since it is increasing,

instead of lifting,

my homesickness.

在阅读英文的过程中，常有《静夜思》之联想，借用英文，不仅语言地道，时有亮点，且可深化诗意，隽永意境。

《李白望月的 150 种方式》，其实，回译自英文书名：*Li Bai: 150 Ways of Looking at the Moon*，而英文书名则受到艾略特·温伯格（Eliot Weinberg）*19 Ways of Looking at Wang Wei*（《观看王维的十九种方式》）的启发。这样的书名，在英语母语读者看来，自然亲切。不过，《李白望月的 150 种方式》，亦可如此英译：150 Variations of *Jingyesi, or Longing for Home in the Dead of Night* by Li Bai，回译汉语，则是：《〈静夜思〉的 150 种变奏曲》，这正是对本书内容的恰当诠释。

海德格尔说："诗人的天职是还乡。"

我说:"汉诗英译者的天职,是送给西方一轮中国的月亮。"

然而,唐人张九龄《望月怀远》,早有预言:

"不堪盈手赠,还寝梦佳期。"

何故?

中国的月亮,

当然,远比西方的

圆。

在这本有点个性的小书中,笔者画了——若加上前述 10 种英译——160 个圆月。当然,不是圆规画出的绝对的圆月,而是艺术的圆月。圆规之月,是小学生画出的月亮;艺术之月,小学生一般看不懂的——为什么要这么画呢?

长大有梦或初醒,憬然彻悟惊复惊。

半扇门楣裱真情,译诗岂是苟苟营?

《静夜思》如何英译?中国古典诗歌如何英译?

这——

是我们人类根本的问题。

大约一周前,在英译《静夜思》的过程中,竟写出一首小诗,诗题同名《静夜思》,以此作为《静夜思》无法结束的结束吧:

静夜思

静极——

谁人在思?

风雪夜,

归人何处?

天地间,

飘飘何物?

似沙,

若鸥……

张智中

2024 年 2 月 4 日初稿

2024 年 2 月 21 日修订

津门松间居

著名诗人、书法家王猛仁书法

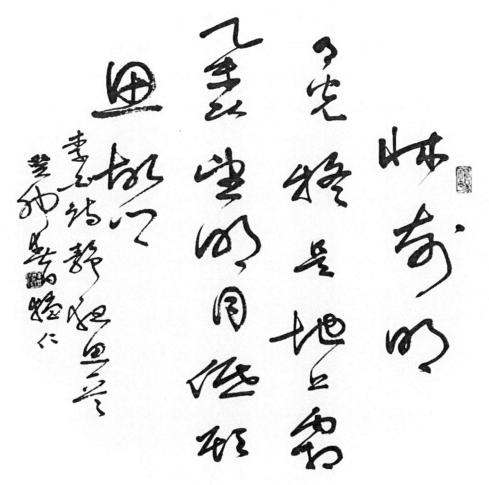

著名神性诗人李青淞书法

目

次

望月之 1：Pining in a Quiet Night（思念在静夜）

读英文

She was **pining** for her mother.
她思念著母亲。

She certainly hasn't been **pining** while you were away.
你不在的时候她可并不难受。

I woke **in the night.**
我夜里醒了。

I **doubt** if it's true.
我看这未必是事实。

She blushed and hastily **lowered** her eyes.
她脸一红，匆忙垂下了眼睛。

英文散译

Pining in a Quiet Night

Before bed bright moonlight, doubted as frost on the ground. Raising head, see a bright moon; lowering head, think of hometown.

英文诗译

Pining in a Quiet Night

Before bed bright moonlight,

doubted as frost on the ground.
Raising head, see a bright moon;
lowering head, think of hometown.

回译

思念在静夜
前床明月光，
疑是霜地上。
举头见明月，
低头想故乡。

译人语

显然，只是两个地方字词的顺序颠倒了："床前"，变成了"前床"；"地上霜"，变成了"霜地上"。这种直译或字译的方法，虽然显得刻板，却也是古诗英译之一法，在古诗英译中也是一个流派。以前有，至今仍有。这种翻译策略，国内译者少用，海外译者常见。好处是，可让西方读者感受到汉语或汉语诗歌的样子，所谓原汁原味。弊端也很明显，不利于诗情诗意的充分发挥和淋漓再现。

另外，注意每行第一个单词首字母的大小写问题。如果每行第一个单词的首字母一律大写，是英语诗歌的传统做法。这里的译文中，偶行首单词的首字母没有大写，是当代英诗的习惯做法。总体而言，追求通俗易懂，追求诗歌的散文化，是当代诗歌的一个趋势。如上英译，若不分行，则是散文：

Before bed bright moonlight, doubted as frost on the ground. Raising head, see a bright moon; lowering head, think of hometown.

字母的大小写不变的。

《静夜思》采取直译法，笔者有另一译文，与此大体类似，兹录于此，不再另述。

Quiet Night Longing

Before bed bright moonlight
is taken as frost aground.
Lift head to look at the moon;

lower head to long for home.

若散文读之，则更易理解：

Before bed bright moonlight is taken as frost aground. Lift head to look at the moon; lower head to long for home.

这里，is taken as 似比 doubted as 更加灵活到位。另外，"思乡"，以 long for home 出之，明白练达。

望月之 2：Missing in the Dead of Night（思念在深夜）

读英文

I **miss** you terribly!
我多么想你呀！

His behavior was **suggestive** of a cultured man.
他的举止显示出他是个有教养的人。

Suddenly the young woman **raised her eyes** and saw something brown in the branches.
突然，这个年轻的女子抬头看到树枝里有一个棕色的东西。

The thought of Dounia and his mother suddenly **reduced** him almost **to** a panic.
一想到都丽娅和他的母亲，突然迫使他有一种恐惧感。

But he had seen the man **reduce** the toughest landlords **to** jelly.
但他见过老板把最难缠的房东收拾得服服帖帖。

After one year's illness he was **reduced** to a skeleton.
他病了一年之后瘦得像个骷髅。

It was my lot almost every day to make discoveries which **reduced** me almost **to** despair.
几乎每天都有新的发现，搞得我天天闷闷不乐的。

英文散译

Missing in the Dead of Night

A moonbeam shoots through the window, which is suggestive of frost on the ground. Raising my eyes toward the bright moon, I am reduced to homesickness soon.

英文诗译

Missing in the Dead of Night

A moonbeam shoots through the window,

which is suggestive of frost on the ground.

Raising my eyes toward the bright moon,

I am reduced to homesickness soon.

回译

思念在深夜
一束光线透过窗户射入，
令人想起大地之霜。抬
望眼，明月高悬，我不
禁黯然，思乡之情顿生。

译人语

不追求押尾韵的自由体译诗，最大的好处，是译者可以不受拘束，充分正确地表达原诗的意思，而不至于译出一些为押韵而导致不堪卒读或令读者不知所云的文字来。本来，任何类型的翻译，通顺流畅，都是基本的要求。

在考察汉诗译英译的质量之时，其实，我们有个可行的方法，就是把英译后的诗歌，做散文排列，以观其流畅效果。那么，来看英译散读：

A moonbeam shoots through the window, which is suggestive of frost on the ground. Raising my eyes toward the bright moon, I am reduced to homesickness soon.

考察译文质量的另一个方法，就是回译法。那么，上面英译回译成汉语，散文排列，则是：

　　一束光线透过窗户射入，令人想起大地之霜。抬望眼，明月高悬，我不禁黯然，思乡之情顿生。

做诗行排列，则是如上之回译。

回译虽然采取散文的语言，却采取豆腐块似的整齐，而且，第二行中间使用了句号，行尾却没有标点，形成典型的跨行。

与李白原诗相比，译文比较中规中矩。

"举头望明月"，英译 Raising my eyes toward the bright moon："头"，变成了"眼"（eyes）；动词"望"，变成了介词"朝向"（toward），符合英文表达。

唯"低头"之信息失落——可乎？其实，"举头"、"低头"中外译家一般都照直译出，有时亦可，有时则不免滑稽，令英文读者另做他想。如有译作：head up ... head down ... 中国学者捧为神来之笔，西方读者却感觉在做俯卧撑，有眩晕之感。如此中西读者之巨大差异，不可不考。

在我们看来，"举头"、"低头"只是一种艺术之符号，大可不必当真。因此，这里"低头"没有字译，似乎不必大惊小怪。况且，译文中的动词 reduced 及其回译"黯然"，不是已经译出了"低头"的内在情感了吗？

"举头望明月，低头思故乡"，犹如"才上眉头，却下心头"，所谓"举头"、"低头"，正是诗人内心无法言说的许多东西。俯仰之间，饱含了诗人内心丰沛的情感。在这千古流传的五绝经典中，"举头"、"低头"，正是一种艺术符号，通过这种艺术符号，诗人用间接的方式传达出他内心无法说出的东西。

自由体译诗，可以忠实于原诗的行数及其长短，只是放弃尾韵而已。当然，也可不必拘泥于原诗的行数，译者根据诗情做随意——随着诗意——的增加或减少。当然，因为汉语古诗的精炼省净，一般都是增加诗行，而不是减少诗行。

望月之 3：Still Night Yearning （静夜的渴望）

读英文

Frosty windows make great surfaces for children to draw on.
有霜的窗户是孩子们画画的好地方。

Her steady **gaze** did not waver.
她目不转睛地注视著。

The compact **disc** is a miracle of modern technology.
激光唱片是当代技术的奇葩。

Across the bay the moon was a luminous **disc** in ther western sky.
一轮明月挂在海湾对面的西天上。

Mark's eyes **were alight with** excitement.
马克的眼里闪烁着激动的光。

His face **was alight with** anger.
他满脸愠怒的神色。

英文散译

Still Night Yearning

The bedside floor is frosty with a beam of moonlight; I lift my gaze to the disc: my face for home is alight.

英文诗译

Still Night Yearning

The bedside floor is frosty

with a beam of moonlight;

I lift my gaze to the disc:

my face for home is alight.

回译

静夜的渴望

床边的地上如霜，

一道明亮的月光。

抬眼看向那圆盘，

脸上写满着思乡。

译人语

译诗标题，Still Night Yearning, 恰吻合"静夜思"，直译而佳。译文中，系动词 is 加上形容词 frosty，后跟介词 with，是一种常见的富有诗意的表达方式。英文单词 disc，本为"圆盘、盘状物"之意，词典上给出短语：the moon's disc，"月轮"之意。这里，disc 独用，在上下文中，含义也非常清楚了。最后一行：my face for home is alight. 采取了倒装，正常语序是：my face is alight for home。四行整齐，偶行单词 moonlight 与 alight，押完美韵。回译也诗行整齐划一，尾韵铿锵。可谓格律体译诗。

另外，此诗虽然简单，明白如话，"疑是地上霜"中的"疑是"，如果理解成"怀疑是"，也不算错，例如《激发孩子想象力的古诗 100 首》（戴建业著，复旦大学出版社，2021 年）177 页注释："疑是：以为是。疑：怀疑，疑惑。"但似乎缺少点诗意。最近读到《风月同天：日本人眼中最美中国古诗 100 首》（李均洋，（日）佐藤利行，荣喜朝主编，人民文学出版社，2020 年）19 页的注释："疑是：好像是，简直就是。"感觉这样理解更为合理，至少更加富有诗意。不过，本译采用 is frosty with（"地上如霜"）来表达，避开了这个问题，却同样诗意盎然。

望月之 4：Moonward & Homeward（向月·向家）

读英文

Moonlight was my **homeward** escort.
月光是我归途上的护卫人。

She walked with her shoulders back and her nose pointing **skyward**.
她抬头挺胸，鼻孔朝天地走。

The garden **is bright with** sunshine.
花园里阳光灿烂。

Her eyes **are bright with** interest.
她眼中闪着好奇的光彩。

His **thoughts** seemed to be jumbled up.
他的思想似乎很混乱。

英文散译

Moonward & Homeward

The floor with moonlight is frostily bright — lifting gaze moonward, thoughts flying homeward….

英文诗译

Moonward & Homeward

The floor with moonlight

is frostily bright —

lifting gaze moonward,

thoughts flying homeward….

回译

向月·向家

地上的月光

霜一般明亮——

抬头向月，

思想向家，飞翔……

译人语

"床前"，变成"地上"（floor），接下来，with moonlight is frostily bright 是倒装，正常语序是：The floor is frostily bright with moonlight（地面由于月光，变得像霜一样明亮。）名词"霜"，英译用 frostily，从名词到副词，看似简单，其实，这样使用，更加符合英文的行文习惯。

动词"望"和"思"，也词性转变，用了副词 moonward 和 homeward，分别作为第三行和第四行的尾词，押同音韵；一、二行 moonlight 和 bright 也押完美韵。整首译诗韵式：aabb。四个诗行，虽长短不一，却每行 5 个音节，可谓格律体译诗，含机巧之运思。

回顾标题：Moonward & Homeward，中间的符号&，虽大意等同 and，却更表两者密切之关系。回译标题《向月·向家》，同具诗意。

望月之 5：Still Night Yearning（静夜思）

读英文

She smiled, looking **dreamily** out on the shifty landscape.
她脸露微笑，用一种梦幻似的目光看着那变化莫测的景色。

Alexandra watched the shimmering pool **dreamily**.
亚历山德拉出神地望着波光粼粼的池塘。

His behavior **was suggestive of** a cultured man.
他的举止暗示他是一个有教养的人。

The ground was covered with **hoarfrost** in the early morning.
清早地上盖满了白霜。

They are back again like a **long lost** friend.
它们再次出现，就像久违的老朋友。

英文散译

Still Night Yearning

The floor is dreamily bright with light of the moon, suggestive of hoarfrost.
Lifting my gaze to the moon so bright, I begin to miss my home long lost.

英文诗译

Still Night Yearning

The floor is dreamily bright with light

of the moon, suggestive of hoarfrost.

Lifting my gaze to the moon so bright,

I begin to miss my home long lost.

回译

静夜思

地面梦幻一般，因月光

——明亮，暗示着白霜。

举目透望，见月亮光光，

我开始想念久违的故乡。

译人语

较之前几种译文，此译稍显冗长。有个别词语的添加使用，如 dreamily（梦幻一般），begin（开始），long lost（久违的）等，这如同胶合剂，将英文单词组合连接成好的句子，以便更好地传达李白静夜思之意。另外，译诗采用 light of the moon，比 the moonlight 稍显冗长，但却带来一种新鲜的感觉，这正是诗歌在措词方面的追求。"疑是"，英文用 suggestive of（暗示着），不失为一种较好的变通。再看标题，Still Night Yearning，正是"静夜思"之直译：简明而新鲜。整体观之，诗行行尾单词：light 与 bright，hoarfrost 与 lost，押交叉韵；每行 9 个音节，可谓格律体译诗。

回译诗题《静夜思》，与原诗题吻合，印证直译之功。回译语言采用口语体，明白畅晓，却形式上整齐划一。原诗之尾韵："光"、"霜"、"乡"不变，但诗的用词却有明显变化。"床前"，变"地面"；"疑是"，变"暗示着"；"举头"，变"举目"；添加较多："梦幻一般"，"开始"，"久违的"，以及主语"我"。同时，"低头"省去——此语虽然重要，却是个艺术符号，表示黯然神伤之意。而思念故乡之淡淡忧伤，早已体现在译文之中去了。无论变词，无论增词，无论减词，不改变原诗之诗意，乃是翻译之要害。

望月之 6：Missing in the Dead of Night（静夜之思念）

读英文

His behavior was **suggestive** of a cultured man.
他的举止暗示他是一个有教养的人。

He **took an upward glance at** the helicopter.
他举目向直升机一瞥。

He would **steal upward glances at** the clock.
他不时偷偷往上看钟。

Their business misfortune had **reduced** the family to a state of total despair, and Gregor's only concern at that time had been to arrange things so that they could all forget about it as quickly as possible.
他们生意上的噩运让全家陷入了彻底的绝望之中。那时，格雷戈尔唯一关心的就是安排好所有事情，好让全家人能够尽快忘掉一切。

The wine and the good dinner had **reduced** my former guardian to silence.
葡萄酒和美食使我的前监护人陷入了沉默。

Homesickness is motivation and destination of his writing.
乡愁是作家写作的动力，亦是写作的归宿。

英文散译

Missing in the Dead of Night

A moonbeam through the window is suggestive of frost on the ground; upward glancing at the bright moon reduces me to homesickness soon.

英文诗译

Missing in the Dead of Night
A moonbeam through the window is
suggestive of frost on the ground;
upward glancing at the bright
moon reduces me to
homesickness
soon.

回译

静夜之思念
透过窗户的一束月光使我
想起大地之上的冷霜
抬望眼：一轮明月
立刻使我沉
浸在乡思
之中

译人语

译诗散读："透过窗户的一束月光，使我想起大地之上的冷霜，抬望眼：一轮明月，立刻使我沉浸在乡思之中。"与第一个译文比较，可见只有一个变化：原译的 Raising my eyes toward the bright moon, I am reduced to homesickness soon 改成了 upward glancing at the bright moon reduces me to homesickness soon。其实，在读英国小说家和诗人哈代的英文诗集时，读到了 upward glancing 这两个单词的组合，便觉得眼前一亮，觉得可用来英译李白之"举头"。在以往众多的英译文中，也有适当变通，把"抬头"译作"抬眼"（raise/lift my eyes）的。这里的 upward glancing，只是"向上的目光"，感觉更贴切更含蓄。另外，原译 Raising my eyes toward the bright moon, I am reduced to homesickness soon，中间有个逗号，由小句和主句组成。改译后的 upward glancing at the bright moon reduces me to homesickness soon，将其合并成一个句子，更具英文味道。英译诗之回译，显然是一首非常现代化的新诗。如果与前引《静夜思》的今译比较，自由体的今译，形式上更放开了，诗情也就容易散发出来。

望月之 7：Homey Scraps Through Moonlight（月光里的乡愁）

读英文

Just **a splash of** milk in my coffee, please.

请在我的咖啡里稍为加点儿牛奶。

A swine overfat is **the cause of** his own bane.

猪因壮死。

It's difficult to pinpoint **the cause of** the accident.

很难清楚地找到事故发生的原因。

Old memory **awakes in me** when I see the picture.

我看到这张照片时，件件往事涌上心头。

I have **a dim recollection of** it.

我依稀记得这事。

Yet the look they envisioned was Old World, rustic and **homey**.

然而，他们所设想的是一个旧世界，质朴的和舒适的。

She broomed up the **scraps** of paper.

她把纸屑扫在一起。

He moved from end to end of his voluptuous bedroom, looking again at the **scraps** of the day's journey that came unbidden into his mind.

他在自己富丽堂皇的卧室里来回走动着，不由自主地回想起白天旅行时遇到的种种情景。

英文散译

Homey Scraps Through Moonlight

I rise in midnight to find a splash of moonlight before my bed — frost on the ground? The cause of my disconsolation is the moon, which awakes in me a recollection of homey scraps ....

英文诗译

Homey Scraps Through Moonlight

I rise in midnight to find a splash of moonlight before my bed — frost on the ground?
The cause of my disconsolation is the moon,
which awakes in me a recollection
of homey scraps ....

回译

月光里的乡愁
半夜醒来，月光洒水
床前——地上之霜？
伤感，都是月亮惹的祸，
唤醒我，内心回忆，
家乡的点滴……

译人语

英译中，disconsolation 为名词，"悲伤；阴暗"之意。除了"读英文"中的借鉴之外，译诗也借鉴了霍克斯英译《红楼梦》第九回中的一个句子：

到了这天，宝玉起来时，袭人早已把书笔文物收拾停妥，坐在床沿上发闷，见宝玉起来，只得伏侍他梳洗。宝玉见他闷闷的，问道："好姐姐，你怎么又不喜欢了？难道怕我上学去，撂的你们冷清了不成？"

When the appointed day arrived, Bao-yu **rose** in the morning **to find** that Aroma had already got his books, brushes and other writing materials ready for him and was sitting **disconsolately** on the side of his bed. Seeing him get up, she roused herself and helped him to do his hair and wash. He asked her **the cause of** her despondency.

'What's upset you this time, Aroma? I can't believe you are worried about being left alone while I am at school.'

以及霍克斯英译《红楼梦》第八回中的一个句子：

宝玉方想起早起的事来，因笑道："我写的那三个字在那里呢？"

Skybright's words **awoke in Bao-yu a recollection of** the morning's events. 'What became of the three characters I wrote?'

汉诗英译，当以借鉴英文原文为主；而好的汉译英中的英文表达，同样值得借鉴，可以用来英译其他汉语文学作品。如此，才称得上是真正成功的汉译英文学作品。

望月之 8：Homesickness in the Depth of Night（**想家在深夜**）

读英文

It happened **in the depth of** winter.
那事发生在隆冬。

He was **in the depths of** despair.
他处于绝望的深渊。

It takes him a long time **to wake from** his night's sleep.
他过了很久才从睡梦中醒来。

She kept lifting handfuls of fine sand and letting it **pour through** her fingers.
她反复的用手抓起细细的沙子，让它们从手指的缝隙漏出。

When I woke, sunlight was already **pouring through** the windows.
当我醒来时，太阳光已经从窗户透射进来。

The treatment given here is **suggestive** rather than thorough.
这里所给出的论述，是提示性的而不是完整的。

He would steal **upward glances at** the clock.
他不时偷偷往上看钟。

His reply **reduced** me **to** silence.
他的回答使我哑口无言。

You almost **reduce** me **to** tears.
你快要让我流下眼泪来了。

—18—

英文散译

Homesickness in the Depth of Night

I wake, in the depth of night, from a dream to find moonlight pouring through the window, into my room, onto the ground, suggestive of frost. Upward looking at the moon reduces me to homesickness soon.

英文诗译

Homesickness in the Depth of Night

I wake, in the depth of night,
from a dream to find moonlight
pouring through the window,
into my room, onto the ground,
suggestive of frost. Upward
looking at the moon reduces
me to homesickness soon.

回译

想家在深夜
我醒来，深更半夜，
从梦中，只见月光
朗照着流泻，透窗户，
入房间，照地上，
疑是地上之霜。抬头
望一眼明月，我
便马上开始思乡。

译人语

英译中，I wake, in the depth of night, from a dream to find moonlight pouring through the window, into my room …，也借鉴了美国著名散文家怀特（E. B. White）散文中的一个句子：

Once, when I was a child, I waked from a bad dream to find moonlight pouring into the room, falling across my face like the flashlight of a prowler.

　　有时，英译借鉴一个英文单词或短语；有时则借鉴一个英文句子或句子结构。此译中，…pouring through …, into…, onto….三个介词的使用，动态感得以强化。译诗之时，想起了张若虚《春江花月夜》中"愿逐月华流照君"的句子。

望月之 9：Missing in the Dead of Night （静夜之思）

读英文

We **awakened** to find the others had gone.
我们醒来发觉其他人已经走了。

He was too weak even to **lift** his hand.
他虚弱得连手都抬不起来。

There was **a touch of** sarcasm in her voice.
她的话音中有点儿讥讽的意味。

But I did not care. I felt a great curiosity **come over** me.
然我却毫不在意，我感到一阵巨大的好奇心攫住了我。

On hearing of the victory, the nation was **transported** with joy.
听到胜利的消息，全国人民喜不自胜。

英文散译

Missing in the Dead of Night

Midnight sees me being awakened by a pool of silvery light, which is suggestive of cold frost. I lift my eyes to the window, where moonlight comes in, a dreamy beam, and a touch of nostalgia comes over me, transporting me to my distant homeland, my dear home.

英文诗译

Missing in the Dead of Night
Midnight sees me being awakened
by a pool of silvery light, which
is suggestive of cold frost.
I lift my eyes to the window,
where moonlight comes in,
a dreamy beam, and a touch
of nostalgia comes over me,
transporting me to my distant
homeland, my dear home.

回译

静夜之思
夜半三更见我醒
一池银光，令人
想起冷霜。
我抬头看窗，
月光如注，
梦幻般的光束，一丝
乡愁袭心头，
带我神游遥远的
故乡，亲爱的家乡。

译人语

英译中，where moonlight comes in, a dreamy beam ....，借用了劳伦斯名著《恋爱中的女人》（*Women in Love*）中的句子：

The cages were all placed round a small square window at the back, where sunshine came in, a beautiful beam, filtering through green leaves of a tree. （笼子在一扇小四方窗后摆成一圈儿，阳光穿过树木婆娑的绿叶，透过小窗，撒落下来。）

英译中，and a touch of nostalgia comes over me, transporting me to my distant homeland, my dear home, 借用了劳伦斯名著《恋爱中的女人》（*Women in Love*）中的句子：

But the nostalgia came over her, she must be among the people.（但是她的心对这里有一种留恋，她必须呆在这些人之中。）

英译中，transporting me to my distant homeland，其中动词 transport，含有"使（某人）充满强烈情感（尤指快乐）"之意。

望月之 10：Longing for Home in the Dead of Night（静谧之夜，想家……）

读英文

When people are too well off they always begin to **long for** something new.
当人们太富有时，他们总是开始渴望一些新的东西。

All three incidents occurred **in the dead of night**.
三起事件都发生在深夜。

He **cast** a furtive glance at her.
他偷偷瞥了她一眼。

The fire **cast** a ruddy glow over the city.
这场火把城市上空映得一片通红。

It **gives rise to** controversy among experts.
这引起了专家们的争议。

He waited for her arrival in **a fever of** impatience.
他焦急不安地等待她的到来。

英文散译

Longing for Home in the Dead of Night

A white beam is cast upon the ground before my bed, which is suggestive of frost. Upward glancing at the bright moon gives rise to a fever of longing, which transports me far away, to my sweet homeland, my sweet home ....

英文诗译

Longing for Home in the Dead of Night

A white beam is cast

upon the ground

before my bed, which

is suggestive of frost.

Upward glancing

at the bright moon

gives rise to

a fever of longing,

which transports me

far away, to my sweet

homeland, my sweet

home ....

回译

静谧之夜，想家……
一束白色的亮光
投射在床前
的地上，令人
想起夜晚的冷霜。
抬望眼，一轮
明月高挂；
想家的思绪，
油然而生——
一阵思念带我
远去，回到可爱的
家乡，可爱的
家……

译人语

英译中，A white beam is cast upon the ground before my bed，借鉴自如下英

文句子：

The daylight cast a white beam upon the bed.（一束明亮的日光投射在床上。）

英译中，upward glancing at the bright moon gives rise to a fever of longing, which transports me far away, to my sweet homeland, my sweet home ....。其中，a fever of longing（一阵思家之情）的表达，以及英文单词 homeland 与 home 的并用，深有余味。译文借用了英国著名小说家兼诗人哈代（Thomas Hardy）诗歌中的搭配：upward glancing。

以及如下英文句子：

Alone in her hotel room, a fever of longing transported her to her bedroom at home.（她独自一人在旅馆房间里，一阵思家之情似乎把她带到了家中的卧室。）

望月之 11：Missing in the Dead of Night（**静夜思念**）

读英文

The **moonbeam** breaks through rifted clouds.

月光穿过云层缝隙照射下来。

The fingers were gnarled, lumpy, with long, curving nails **suggestive** of animal claws.

那些手指粗糙、不平，有着又长又弯的使人想起动物爪子的指甲。

And as I **lift my eyes** again, I see rows upon rows of roofs, miles of them, stretching in ugly square outlines to the distance.

当我再仰首眺望时，我看见一列一列的屋顶，连结几英里远，形成一些难看的四方形的轮廓，一直伸展到远方去。

Tourists throng the place to **get a glimpse of** the ruins of this beautiful city.

旅游者蜂拥而至，以便一睹这座美丽城市的废墟。

After five minutes the music fades, lights dim, and baby can **drift off to** dreamland.

五分钟后音乐慢慢消逝，灯光变暗，宝宝能进入梦乡。

She was so tired, her eyelids were beginning to **droop**.

她太疲倦了，眼睑开始往下垂。

Not all problems **arising** from social discrimination can be addressed through communication.

并不是所有由社会歧视引起的问题都可以通过沟通来解决。

英文散译

Missing in the Dead of Night

A moonbeam through the window is suggestive of frost on the ground. When I lift my eyes to get a glimpse of the bright moon, my mind drifts off to my distant homeland and, I droop my neck in sorrow, nostalgia arising.

英文诗译

Missing in the Dead of Night

A moonbeam through the window
is suggestive of frost on the ground.
When I lift my eyes to get a glimpse
of the bright moon, my mind drifts
off to my distant homeland and,
I droop my neck in sorrow,
nostalgia arising.

回译

静夜思念
一束光线透过窗户射入，
令人想起大地之霜。
抬望眼，只见
一轮明月，我的思想飞回
遥远的故乡——
我垂头丧气，思乡
之情油然而生。

译人语

在此译文中，"举头"、"低头"似有明显的传译。而相关的英文措词，仍与英文阅读有关。在 Rupi Kaur 所著诗集 *The Sun and Her Flowers*（2017 年

Andrews McMeel Publishing 出版，Kansas City, Missouri）中，我们读到这样的句子：

"only then / can my mind / drift off to sleep"，由此衍化出译诗中 my mind drifts off to my distant homeland 的句子；

"I could not lift my eyes / to meet eyes with someone else"，由此衍化出译诗中 When I lift my eyes to get a glimpse of the bright moon 的句子；

"the cranes will droop their necks in sorrow"，由此衍化出译诗中 I droop my neck in sorrow, nostalgia arising 的句子。当然，这里的表述，"低下脖子"，是"低头"的适当变通。如果不是阅读英文，一般很难想起这样的表述。

另外，英文译诗中，my mind drifts off to my distant homeland and, I droop my neck in sorrow, nostalgia arising，连词 and 之后使用逗号，其实在英文文学作品中常见。例如英国著名作家詹姆斯·乔伊斯（James Joyce）《都柏林人》（Dubliners）中的这个句子：

He looked down the slope and, at the base, in the shadow of the wall of the Park, he saw some human figures lying.（他朝山坡下望去，山脚处，在公园围墙的阴影里，他隐约看到有些人躺在那里。）

在连词 and 之后，使用逗号，可调节语言的节奏和语气。整体观之，原诗四行，译诗七行，在诗行数字上有变化，但在内容上变化幅度不大，可谓基本忠实的译文。

望月之 12：Longing in the Stillness of Night（**静夜渴望**）

读英文

In the stillness of night could be heard the ringing of a distant bell.
更深人静的时候，可以听到远处的钟声。

In daylight he can't imagine it in darkness **with moonlight seeping through the cracks**.
在白天，他不能想象黑暗中的情形：月光穿过缝隙而来。

Instead, I see Twelve Oaks and remember **how the moonlight slants across the white columns**, and the unearthly way the magnolias look, opening under the moon, and how the climbing roses make the side porch shady even at the hottest noon.
另一方面，我却看见了"十二橡树"村，回想月光怎样从那些白柱子中间斜照过来，山茱萸花在月色中开得那样美，茂密的蔷薇藤把走廊一侧荫蔽得使最热的中午也显得那样清凉。

The cream-colored walls glowed with light and the depths of the mahogany furniture **gleamed** deep red like wine, while the floor **glistened** as if it were glass, except where the rag rugs covered it and they were spots of gay color.
……使那些奶油色墙壁都闪闪发亮，桃花心木家具也泛出葡萄酒一般深红的光辉，地板也像玻璃似的耀眼，让连沿着旧地毯的地方也洒满了灰色光点。

She looked at him with **lingering**, friendly eyes.

她的眼睛望着沃丁顿，目光友善，久未移开。

And, of course, Melly and I **are longing to see the dear baby**.

并且，当然喽，媚兰和我都急于想看看那个亲爱的小乖乖。

英文散译

Longing in the Stillness of Night

In my bed with moonlight seeping and slanting through the window, before streaming brilliantly into my room, the floor gleams and glistens silvery like frost. I look up with a long, slow, reflective look, in gloomy, heavy silence, at the moon which, slipping momentarily into my sight, is shining clearly, lingeringly overhead, and I am longing to see my dear home, my dear land.

英文诗译

Longing in the Stillness of Night

In my bed with moonlight seeping and slanting

through the window, before streaming brilliantly

into my room, the floor gleams and glistens silvery

like frost. I look up with a long, slow, reflective look,

in gloomy, heavy silence, at the moon which, slipping

momentarily into my sight, is shining clearly, lingeringly

overhead, and I am longing

to see my dear home,

my dear land.

回译

静夜渴望

我躺在床上，斜斜的月光从窗户

渗入，之后灿灿地泄入

我的房间。地上闪闪烁烁，

如银似霜。我抬眼望去，目光缓慢、悠长，

若有所思，死寂、沉郁，月亮时不时地

滑入我的视野，其光灿灿，于清空
徘徊——渴望骤生：
吾爱吾家，吾爱
吾乡。

译人语

英译中，with moonlight seeping and slanting through the window, before streaming brilliantly into my room，除了"读英文"中的句子外，还借鉴了如下两个英文句子：

Lying in the bed with the moonlight streaming dimly over her, she pictured the whole scene in her mind.（躺在床上，她全身沐浴着朦胧的月光，心里揣摩着通盘的情景。）

The day was warm for April and the golden sunlight streamed brilliantly into Scarlett's room through the blue curtains of the wide windows.（那是暖和的四月天，金色的阳光穿过宽大的窗户上的天蓝色帷帘灿烂地照入思嘉的房间。）

英译中，I look up with a long, slow, reflective look, in gloomy, heavy silence，借鉴如下英文类似的英文表达：

… a reflective look on her face.（……而是若有所思的表情。）

Martha looked reflective again.（玛莎看上去又若有所思了。）

She looked at him with a long, slow look, malevolent, supercilious.（郝麦妮缓缓地审视了他很久，那目光恶毒、傲慢。）

She looked at him with a long, slow inscrutable look, as he stood before her negligently, the water standing in beads all over his skin.（戈珍缓缓地把目光投向他，眼神怪异地看着他。他大大咧咧地站在她面前，皮肤上泛着水珠。）

She stood looking at him in gloomy, heavy silence, for some time.（她沉郁、默默地看了他一会儿。）

英译中，at the moon which, slipping momentarily into my sight，借鉴如下英文：

In the movie version of events, all is almost lost when the moon slips momentarily out of sight, only to suddenly reappear at the last moment, proving that their realignment was successful.

英译中，... is shining clearly, lingeringly overhead, and I am longing to see my dear home, my dear land，除了"读英文"中的句子外，还借鉴了如下两个英文句子：

The moon shone clearly overhead, with almost impertinent brightness, the small dark boats clustered on the water, there were voices and subdued shouts.

The horses, feeling slack reins, stretched down their necks to crop the tender spring grass, and the patient hounds lay down again in the soft red dust and looked up longingly at the chimney swallows circling in the gathering dusk.（两骑马觉得缰绳松了，便伸长脖子去啃柔嫩的春草，猎犬们重新在灰土中躺下，贪馋地仰望着在愈来愈浓的暮色中回旋飞舞的燕子。）

望月之 13：Nostalgia in the Depth of the Night（**深夜乡思**）

读英文

Listening to classical music, especially **in the depth of night**, makes my mind travel around the world, bathed in the soft breeze and bright moonlight of great nature.

听古典音乐，尤其在深夜，能使我的心灵遨游世界，陶醉在大自然的轻风和明月里。

Then, the decision made, she looked at him **sharply**.

然后，她心意已决，目光锐利地看着吉姆。

Up here on the hill a few glowworms were **lighting up**.

小镇山丘上只有几只萤火虫，在暗自地散发着淡冷色的光芒。

They toiled on a **small patch** of land.

他们在一小块土地上劳作。

They **close around** the casualty and I leave with Fiona.

他们紧密围绕着伤员开始施救，我和菲奥娜离开了手术室。

They built a moat to **encompass** the castle.

他们在城堡周围修了一条护城河。

英文散译

Nostalgia in the Depth of the Night

Here and there, the moonlight comes in sharply through window panes, lighting up small patches on the floor of my bedroom, which are suggestive of frost. It seems nostalgia is closing around, to encompass me, and my mind is transported to the distant land of my home, my sweet home ....

英文诗译

Nostalgia in the Depth of the Night
Here and there, the moonlight comes in sharply
through window panes, lighting up small patches
on the floor of my bedroom, which are
suggestive of frost. It seems nostalgia
is closing around, to encompass me,
and my mind is transported
to the distant land of my
home, my sweet
home ....

回译

深夜乡思
这儿，那儿，亮堂堂的月光
透过窗户的格子，在卧室
的地面点亮小块小块
如霜的光斑。乡愁
四合，将我包围，
我的心思飞回
遥远的故乡，
甜蜜的家
乡……

译人语

英译中，Here and there, the moonlight comes in sharply through window panes, lighting up small patches on the floor 借鉴如下译文句子：

After the brightness of the day outside, the interior of the cottage seemed cool and dark. Here and there, the sun came in sharply through narrow gaps, lighting up small patches on the tatami. （从亮晃晃的外头进来，小屋里似乎又冷又暗。阳光从各处狭窄的缝隙里强烈地照射进来，在榻榻米上投下一个个小光斑。）

英译中，It seems nostalgia is closing around, to encompass me 借鉴下面两个英文句子：

Darkness encompassed them. （黑暗包裹着他们。）

Darkness closed around, and then came the ringing of church bells. （暮色四合，紧接着传来了教堂的钟声。）

望月之 14：An Ache for Home in the Deep Night（**深夜想家**）

读英文

Being away from home for a long time, I always **ache for** home.
离开家乡很久了，我常常想家。

He **was dazzled by** her beauty and wit.
她聪明貌美使他为之神魂颠倒。

A shaft of moonlight fell on the lake.
一束月光照在湖面上。

The needle **pierced** her finger.
针刺进了她的手指。

They **were drowned in** riot all night.
他们通宵沉浸在狂欢之中。

A sense of futility stole over her.
一种没用的感觉向她袭来。

The pain immediately **eased**.
疼痛立刻减轻了。

英文散译

An Ache for Home in the Deep Night
Suddenly I am dazzled by a frost-like shaft of moonlight that pierces the

window panes and falls directly on to the ground by my bed, and I am drowned in the pool of light, in homesickness, where I feel a sense of loss and a kind of ache I do not know how to name it — an ache for home, which can be eased in no way.

英文诗译

An Ache for Home in the Deep Night

Suddenly I am dazzled by a frost-like shaft of moonlight

that pierces the window panes and falls directly on

to the ground by my bed, and I am drowned in

the pool of light, in homesickness, where I

feel a sense of loss and a kind of ache

I do not know how to name it —

an ache for home, which

can be eased

in no way.

回译

深夜想家

突然，我眩晕于一束冷霜一样的月光——

光束刺穿窗户的方格，直射到

我床前的地面上。一屋子的月光，

淹没了我；乡愁，淹没了我。

惶兮惑兮，若有所失，若有

所痛；莫名其失，莫名

其痛。我痛，我痛啊，

我的家——此痛无计

可消除。

译人语

英译中，Suddenly I am dazzled by a shaft of moonlight that pierces the window panes and falls directly on to the ground by my bed 借鉴自下面英文句子：

Suddenly I was dazzled by a shaft of sunlight that pierced the gilt-edged clouds and fell directly on to the Castle.

英译中，which can be eased in no way 中的动词 ease，虽与形容词 easy 相关，但 easy 容易理解，ease 却费思量。动词 ease 的汉语意思，大概是"减轻；放松；缓和；缓慢移动"等，其实，ease 的很多用法非常微妙，不是词典上的解释可以涵盖的。细读如下英文，或可助益：

She eased herself into a chair.（她轻手轻脚地坐到椅子上。）

She eased her injured foot into her shoe.（她小心翼翼地把受伤的脚伸进鞋里。）

I eased my way toward the door.（我缓慢地向门口走去。）

Give me something to ease my pain.（给我些东西，减轻我的痛苦。）

She closed her eyes, allowing my mother to work on them. She drew a breath and eased lower into the bed.（她又闭上眼睛，这样妈妈就可以继续给她化妆。她吸了口气，头陷到枕头里。）

It was the third day of Niki's visit and the rain had eased to a drizzle. I had not been out of the house for several days and enjoyed the feel of the air as we stepped into the winding lane outside.（那是妮基来的第三天，雨小了，变成毛毛细雨。我有几天没有出门了，走在蜿蜒的小路上，户外的空气令我神清气爽。）

She eased her hand from Harold's and pushed back her chair.（她轻轻挣开哈德罗的手，将椅子后挪了一下。）

And perhaps dear Scarlett could find some ease for her sorrow, as Melly is doing, by nursing our brave boys in the hospitals here.（而且亲爱的思嘉也许在这里能找到某种消愁解忧的办法。比如，看护这边医院的勇敢的小伙子们，就像媚兰那样。）

至此，可知英译 an ache for home, which can be eased in no way 中动词 ease 之妙。

另外，译文中采用的 an ache for home，简单有力。这在翁显良《静夜思》的英译中，也有另类妙用（《古诗英译》，翁显良译，北京出版社 1985 年，第 19 页）：

Nostalgia

Li Bai

A splash of white on my bedroom floor. Hoarfrost?

I raise my eyes to the moon, the same moon.

As scenes long past come to mind, my eyes fall again on the splash of white, and my heart aches for home.

望月之 15：Thought in a Moonlit Night（月夜思念）

读英文

They came out into a **moonlit** night heavy with flower scent.
他们出来，走到带着浓郁花香的月光下的夜色中。

The morning light was **stealing through** the shutters.
晨光悄悄穿过了百页窗。

Never copy foreign things blindly or **mechanically**.
不要盲目地或机械地照搬外国的东西。

It's the letters that come out of this exotic place that first **catch their attention**.
这些来自异国他乡的信件最先引起了他们的注意。

The light of the street, no longer dimmed by the dusty glass, **fell full upon his face**.
街上的灯光不再受灰尘仆仆的玻璃遮挡，把他那张脸照得清清楚楚。

Magnus and Annixter joined the group wondering, and all at once **fell full upon** the first scene of a drama.
曼克奈斯和安尼克斯特走进那个人堆里去，心里纳罕着，可是一眨睛工夫就清清楚楚的看到了一出戏的第一幕。

The man seemed to **be beside himself with excitement**.
这人似乎兴奋得忘乎所以。

There was **a touch of** sarcasm in her voice.

她的话音中有点儿讥讽的意味。

How will these changes **affect** us?

这些变化对我们会有什么影响？

It sprang to a gale which now and then, from a tattered sky, flung **pale sweeps of sunlight** over a landscape chaotically tossed.

破絮似的天空时而刮开一块儿，透出一片淡淡的阳光，照着乱纷纷的山水。

Day by day, after the December snows were over, a blazing blue **sky poured down torrents of light and air on the white landscape, which** gave them back in an intenser glitter.

十二月的雪季过了之后，一天又一天，蔚蓝的晴空向地面倾泻光明和空气，雪白的地面又更强更烈地把它们送回。

It doesn't look like such a **moonscape**.

它看起来不再象月球的表面样了。

英文散译

Thought in a Moonlit Night

A moonbeam steals through the window and shines straight on to my bed; at waking, I gaze mechanically at the bright moon, which catches my attention. The silvery light of the moon, filling the air with flying frost, falls full upon my face: I seem to be beside myself with a touch of nostalgia. As the night deepens, the moon affects me more deeply — over the land of my home there are pale sweeps of moonlight, the night sky pouring down torrents of air and moonlight on the boundless landscape which merges with the moonscape.

英文诗译

Thought in a Moonlit Night

A moonbeam steals through the window and shines straight
on to my bed; at waking, I gaze mechanically at the bright
moon, which catches my attention. The silvery light of

the moon, filling the air with flying frost, falls full

upon my face: I seem to be beside myself with

a touch of nostalgia. As the night deepens,

the moon affects me more deeply —

over the land of my home there are

pale sweeps of moonlight, the night

sky pouring down torrents of air

and moonlight on the boundless

landscape which merges

with the moonscape.

回译

月夜思念
一束月光悄悄溜进窗户，径直
照我床上。梦中醒来，我下意识地凝视着
一轮明月，聚精而会神。空中充满
流霜：月之银光晃动，朗照在我
脸上——乡愁袭来，我不能
自已。夜，渐深渐沉；
月，撼心感人——
在家乡广袤的土地上，
淡淡的月光一阵一阵。夜空
倾倒着月光与清气
之激流：风景，其
无边兮；月景，融合
而为一。

译人语

英译中，A moonbeam steals through the window and shines straight on to my bed，借鉴如下英文：

A sunbeam stole through the crack between the window and the black-out curtains and shone straight on to my bed.

英译中，at waking 借鉴如下英文：

Impatient for the light of spring, I have slept lately with my blind drawn up, so that at waking, I have the sky in view.

英译中，I gaze mechanically at the bright moon, which catches my attention 借鉴如下英文：

Bending over the water, he gazed mechanically at the last pink flush of the sunset, at the row of houses growing dark in the gathering twilight. At one distant attic window on the left bank, flashing as though on fire in the last rays of the setting sun, at the darkening water of the canal, and the water seemed to catch his attention. （他俯身望着河水，无意识地凝视着最后一抹粉红色的落日余晖，凝望着在暮色的苍茫中变得越来越黑暗的一排排房屋，凝视着左岸远处阁楼上的一个在闪着红光的窗户，好像在落日的最后一抹余晖中着了火似的，凝望着运河里那处于暗淡之中的河水，河水似乎引起了他的注意。）

英译中，As the night deepens, the moon affects me more deeply 借鉴如下英文：

The moon affects her as it does a woman, he thought. （月光能媚惑海洋，正如能迷乱女子一样，他想。）

另外，译诗标题 Thought in a Moonlit Night 中，用 thought，可暗示哲理性的沉思，而不仅仅是一般意义上对家乡的思念。如此译诗，便有了一丝《春江花月夜》的感觉了。

望月之 16：Thought in the Depth of Night（深夜思念）

读英文

A room **flooded with sunlight**.
充满阳光的房间。

She seemed to be standing in **a pool of light**.
她看起来就像是站在一团光中央。

The natural images in the poem are meant to **be suggestive of** realities beyond themselves.
诗中自然景象的描写意在使人联想起那以外的现实。

With **a stab of** shame, Harold remembered.
带着一阵羞愧，哈罗德突然想起来了。

Gnawing hunger **woke** him **with a start**.
从睡梦中饿醒。

A picture surfaced of his mother's dresses scattered through his **childhood home**. He didn't know where it had come from. He glanced at the window, trying **to have a thought that would** smudge the memory.
不知怎么，哈罗德突然想起了儿时的家，母亲的裙子总是扔得到处都是。他瞥向窗外，想想点别的东西。

Could you **refresh my memory**?

你能提醒我一下吗?

It seems already **a distant memory**.
这好像是很久以前的事了。

His body **ached for** food.
他身体的每一寸都在呼唤食物。

英文散译

Thought in the Depth of Night

My room is flooded with a pool of moonlight which is suggestive of frost, and a stab of nostalgia, or gnawing homesickness wakes me with a start in the depth of night. When I glance upward at the bright moon, a picture surfaces of itself with a thought that shortly refreshes my distant memory, transporting me to my dim and distant childhood home, for which my heart and soul is aching ....

英文诗译

Thought in the Depth of Night

My room is flooded with a pool of moonlight which is suggestive
of frost, and a stab of nostalgia, or gnawing homesickness
wakes me with a start in the depth of night. When
I glance upward at the bright moon, a picture
surfaces of itself with a thought that shortly
refreshes my distant memory, transporting
me to my dim and distant childhood home,
for which my heart and soul
is aching

回译

深夜思念
屋内淹着一池的月光——月光
如霜：思乡之痛，如咬如啮。
我半夜惊醒，举目

望月，浮想联翩；

遥远的记忆复活，把我

带到袅袅娜娜如烟

似雾的童年家乡——

我的心，我的魂，

痛着

……

译人语

译文对英文的借鉴中，经常需要对英文做一些微调、合并、融通。比如，英文句子 A room flooded with sunlight 和 She seemed to be standing in a pool of light，借鉴合并之后，便成译文：My room is flooded with a pool of moonlight。再结合英文句子 The natural images in the poem are meant to be suggestive of realities beyond themselves，译文后续 suggestive，成为：My room is flooded with a pool of moonlight which is suggestive of frost。

英文句子 Gnawing hunger woke him with a start 中，gnawing（咬的；痛苦的；折磨人的）很是形象，稍微改动，在英译中使用了 gnawing homesickness。

英文句子 A picture surfaced of his mother's dresses scattered through his childhood home 中，动词 surface（浮现；显露）非常形象，英译 a picture surfaces of itself ...，添加了介词短语 of itself（自行地；自然地），作为动词 surface 的状语，从而使译文更加形象生动。

英文句子 He didn't know where it had come from. He glanced at the window, trying to have a thought that would smudge the memory，其中，to have a thought that，译文改成了 with a thought that。

两个英文句子：Could you refresh my memory? 和 It seems already a distant memory，合并成译文 refreshes my distant memory。

英文句子 His body ached for food，是正常语序，译文为了衔接和连贯，把介词提前，变成 for which my heart and soul is aching ....

简单不变的借鉴，容易；需要变化调适的借鉴，则需要译者较好的语感和娴熟的语言运用能力。

望月之 17：Home-Thoughts in the Still Night, from a Strange Land（静夜乡思，在异乡）

读英文

The summer **light struck into** the corner **brilliantly** in the earlier part of the day.

上午，太阳的光灿烂地照进这个街角。

He spotted a thin ray of **light shining from between** the shutters on the second floor.

从二楼的百叶窗之间，他发现了一条细细的光线。

A heavy, copper-colored beam of **light** came in at the west window, **gilding** the outlines of the children's heads **with** red gold. And **falling** on the wall opposite **in a rich, ruddy illumination**.

一道浓重的橘黄色光线透过西窗射了进来，给孩子们的头上勾勒出一圈火红金黄的轮廓，也给对面的墙壁涂上了一层瑰丽的血红。

"You are fatigued," said madame, **raising her glance** as she knotted the money.

"你累坏了，"老板娘一边包钱打结，一边抬头看了看他说道。

He moved from end to end of his voluptuous bedroom, looking again at the **scraps** of the day's journey that **came unbidden into his mind**.

他在自己富丽堂皇的卧室里来回走动着，不由自主地回想起白天旅行时遇到的种种情景。

英文散译

Home-Thoughts in the Still Night, from a Strange Land

The midnight moonlight strikes into my bedroom brilliantly, when a beam of light is shining from between the window panes, falling on the ground in an illusory, silvery illumination, and gilding it with hoar frost. I, all alone in a strange land, raise my glance at the bright moon which reduces me to homesickness, to home-thoughts, when homey scraps come unbidden into my mind, ticking, tocking, tocking, ticking ....

英文诗译

Home-Thoughts in the Still Night, from a Strange Land

The midnight moonlight strikes into my bedroom brilliantly, when
a beam of light is shining from between the window panes,
falling on the ground in an illusory, silvery illumination,
and gilding it with hoar frost. I, all alone in a
strange land, raise my glance at the bright
moon which reduces me to homesickness,
to home-thoughts, when homey scraps
come unbidden into my mind,
ticking, tocking,
tocking, tick-
ing ....

回译

静夜乡思，在异乡
子夜，灿炫的月光照进我的卧室，一束亮光
穿过窗户格子而来，落在室内的地面上，
其光如梦，似幻；如银，似霜——
涂抹在地表之上。孑然一身，

独处异乡，我举目仰望——
圆月——我伤感油生，思乡
之情奔涌：家的味道，
家的情景，滴滴，
点点，点
点，滴
滴……

译人语

英译诗歌标题：*Home-Thoughts in the Still Night, from a Strange Land*，受到罗伯特·勃朗宁（Robert Browning）的诗作《海外乡思》（*Home-Thoughts, from Abroad*）的启发。李白的《静夜思》，当然也是"乡思"，虽然这种"乡思"不是来自"海外"，而是来自"内陆"。另据《牛津英语搭配词典》（2006 年，外语教学与研究出版社；牛津大学出版社）895 页，关于 land 的搭配：alien / foreign / strange land。例句：She was all alone in a strange land.

英译中，falling on the ground in an illusory, silvery illumination, and gilding it with hoar frost 借鉴自如下英文：A heavy, copper-colored beam of light came in at the west window, gilding the outlines of the children's heads with red gold. And falling on the wall opposite in a rich, ruddy illumination。而措词的顺序等，稍有调整，以适应译诗之整篇。

另外，用 homey scraps 表示"家的味道，家的情景"，措词堪称巧妙。

望月之 18：Inner Recollection in a Moonlit Night（月夜沉思）

读英文

The western end **was** already **bright with moon beams**.
西方上面已为月光照得明亮了。

The snow had ceased, and **a flash of** watery **sunlight** exposed the house on the slope above us in all its plaintive ugliness.
雪已经不下了，淡淡的一闪日光把我们前面山坡上的那所房子的可悲的丑陋暴露无遗。

He **spotted a thin ray of light shining from between the shutters** on the second floor.
从二楼的百叶窗之间，他发现了一条细细的光线。

Lighter and lighter, until at last the sun touched the tops of the still trees, and **poured its radiance over** the hill.
天色越来越亮，最后太阳终于升到了平静的树梢上，把光芒倾洒在山坡上。

Now, the sun was full up, and **movement** began in the village.
这时候太阳已经完全升起来了，村庄开始活跃起来。

I **woke** this morning **out of dreams into** what we call Reality, **into** the daylight.
今晨我自梦中醒来，回到我们所谓的现实中，回到晨光中。

But she was awakened by a loud knocking. At first, since it **was interwoven with the dream from which she was aroused**, she **could not attach the sound to reality**.

她被一阵闹哄哄的敲门声惊醒了。开始她还以为是在做梦，没有意识到敲门声是真的。

It **filled my eyes with its soothing** golden **light**, and my **whole being was warm with its radiance.**

我满眼都是金色的余辉，令人感到惬意，我整个身心都被这光照温暖着。

The sun was low and yellow, sinking down, and in the sky floated a thin, **ineffectual** moon.

金黄的夕阳正在西沉，天上漂浮起一圈淡淡的月影。

It was an afternoon of daydreams; the autumnal light under the low clouds was **propitious to inner recollection**.

这是个充满幻想的午后，秋日的阳光在低低的云彩之下，这样的天气适合内心冥想。

When winter twilight falls in my street with the rain, **a sense of** the horrible sadness of life **descends upon me**.

当冬季的暮色夹着雨点落在我的街道上，我突然深切地感受到生活的悲伤。

On a steaming, **misty** afternoon.

一个烟雾朦胧的下午。

Never did the moon rise with a milder radiance over great London.

升起的月亮以从未如此温柔的光照在伟大的伦敦城。

Who sang "Auld Lang Syne" and howled with sentiment, and more than once **gazed at the full moon through a blur of great, romantic tears**?

那个高歌《友谊地久天长》、伤感而嚎，不止一次透过浪漫的滂沱的泪水朦胧地凝视满月的人吗？

英文散译

Inner Recollection in a Moonlit Night

I am awakened by the moonlight: the room is bright with moon beams when I spot a flash of moonlight, or a thin ray of light shining from between the shutters —

the moon is pouring its radiance over the floor of my bedroom. Illusively, there is movement of frost in the air, when I wake out of dreams into the moonlight. At first, since the moonlight is interwoven with the dream from which I am aroused, I can not attach it to reality. When the moon fills my eyes with its soothing silvery light, it begins to be effectual upon me, and my whole being is warm with its radiance, which is propitious to inner recollection. A sense of homesickness descends upon me — over my homeland, my hometown, my misty hometown which is dim and distant, never does the moon rise with a milder radiance. Again I gaze at the full moon through a blur of great, romantic tears....

英文诗译

Inner Recollection in a Moonlit Night

I am awakened by the moonlight:

the room is bright with moon beams

when I spot a flash of moonlight, or a thin

ray of light shining from between the shutters

— the moon is pouring its radiance over the floor

of my bedroom. Illusively, there is

movement of frost in the air, when I

wake out of dreams into the moonlight.

At first, since the moonlight is interwoven

with the dream from which I am aroused, I can

not attach it to reality. When the

moon fills my eyes with its soothing

silvery light, it begins to be effectual upon

me, and my whole being is warm with its radiance,

which is propitious to inner recollection. A sense of

homesickness descends upon me

— over my homeland, my hometown,

my misty hometown which is dim and distant,

never does the moon rise with a milder radiance.

Again I gaze at the full moon

through a blur of great,

romantic tears....

回译

月夜沉思

我被月光惊醒：

屋子被照得亮堂堂的，

这时我发现一闪月光——一条

细细的光，穿越着百叶之窗。

月亮把光芒倾洒在卧室

的地面上，如梦似幻：

空里流霜不觉飞。

梦醒时分，我置身月光之中

——起初，月光交织于

夜梦，不辨

幻实。当双目

盈满慰藉的

银光，此景，此情，凭何

以堪？其光柔和，吾身温心暖，

不觉神思而冥想矣。乡愁

来袭——夜升之月，从未

如此温柔地朗照在我的家乡，

我的家——淡远迷离飘梦

若雾的，我的家。

透过滂沱的浪漫之泪，我

再度凝视，凝视着，

那一轮满月……

译人语

英译中，I spot a flash of moonlight, or a thin ray of light shining from between the shutters 借鉴自如下两个英文句子：

The snow had ceased, and a flash of watery sunlight exposed the house on the slope above us in all its plaintive ugliness.

He spotted a thin ray of light shining from between the shutters on the second floor.

词语的倒置与合并，显然可见。移花接木也好，移的就箭也好，只为译文更好地表达原文之意。

英译中，it begins to be effectual upon me 借鉴自如下英文句子：

The sun was low and yellow, sinking down, and in the sky floated a thin, ineffectual moon.

英文是否定形式，译文却采用其肯定形式：表达恰好，颇耐涵咏。

此词比较微妙，另如《新英汉词典》中的例子：an effectual remedy：奏效的治疗；《牛津高阶英汉双解词典》中的例子：take effectual action：采取有效行动。

另外，此译用语丰厚，可谓丰厚翻译（thick translation）。或有认为过分者，然，解构之下，译者无需自辩。

望月之 19：Missing in the Silence of Night（思念：在静谧之夜）

读英文

However, a street **light shone outside the window** and **made a pale greenish reflection inside**.

然而，街灯在窗外闪亮，光线投入屋内，反射着淡绿之光。

She **felt queer waking up** in the living-room.

她在客厅里醒来，感觉有点奇怪。

The silence in the room was deep as the night itself.

房间里一片沉寂，一如夜晚之沉寂。

Maureen **stretched back her neck towards the sky, searching the dusk for** the first sprinkle of stars.

莫琳沉思着，转回头，在薄暮里寻找今夜第一颗闪亮的星。

The moonlight was white on the roof next door and the sky was **a gentle summer blue**.

月光照在邻居的屋顶上，白花花的，天空是一片温柔的夏日蓝。

His eyes were fixed on a window on the right side of the second story.

他的眼睛盯着二楼右侧的一个窗户。

The moon **was full and rimmed with a golden light**.

月儿圆满，镶着金边。

The sunlight was **quiet and mellow** in the room.

阳光泄入屋子，安静而柔和。

Time **mellowed** their hard feelings.

时间钝化了他们之间的怒气。

He had to blink several times, trying to lose the pictures, but they still **swam back**.

哈罗德用力眨了几次眼，尝试摆脱那些画面，但它们就是不停地浮现。

The full moon's light was beginning to fade as it sank toward the west.

盈月始亏，向西而沉。

英文散译

Missing in the Silence of Night

A beam of moonlight shines outside the window, which is whitened, and it makes a silvery reflection inside, illuminating the floor before my bed, suggestive of hoarfrost. By myself, I feel queer waking up in the quiet, secret night, where the silence is deep as the night itself. I stretch back my neck towards the sky, now a boundless blue, searching the night for something lost somewhere. I am transfixed, lost in my meditations, when my eyes are fixed on the moon, which is full and rimmed with a golden light, now quiet and mellow in the sky, and the pictures of my childhood home keep swimming back in my mind …. The moon's light is beginning to fade as it sinks toward the west, but my fond memory is not fading ….

英文诗译

Missing in the Silence of Night

A beam of moonlight shines outside the window, which is whitened,
and it makes a silvery reflection inside, illuminating the floor before
my bed, suggestive of hoarfrost. By myself, I feel queer waking up
in the quiet, secret night, where the silence is deep as the night
itself. I stretch back my neck towards the sky, now a boundless
blue, searching the night for something lost somewhere.
I am transfixed, lost in my meditations, when my eyes

are fixed on the moon, which is full and rimmed with

a golden light, now quiet and mellow in the sky,

and the pictures of my childhood home keep

swimming back in my mind …. The moon's

light is beginning to fade as it sinks

toward the west, but my fond

memory is not

fading ….

回译

思念：在静谧之夜

一束月光闪烁，自窗外，白了窗户；屋内，

银色的反光，亮了床前的地上，好像冷霜。

孑然一身，在静秘之夜醒米：夜之静，

一如夜之深。抬头望天，无尽的蓝，

我在夜空中寻觅着，某时，某物。

我呆住了，陷入沉思，望着月亮，

圆圆的，镶着金边，安静于空中，

成熟的模样。我童年家乡的情景，

如潮如涌，在脑海显现……

盈月始亏，向西而沉，

而我内心的美好

记忆，却永不

消褪……

译人语

英译中，I stretch back my neck towards the sky, now a boundless blue, searching the night for something lost somewhere. 借鉴自如下两个英文句子：

Maureen stretched back her neck towards the sky, searching the dusk for the first sprinkle of stars.

The moonlight was white on the roof next door and the sky was a gentle summer blue.

　　显然，译文把第二个句子中的 a gentle summer blue，改成 a boundless blue，而这两个单词恰好押头韵，然后插入第一个英文句子的逗号之后，再接续其后的现在分词短语。这样一来，译文虽然与第一个英文句子大体雷同，但插入了一个短语，便更具有英文之味道了。

　　此译如电影之特写镜头，将《静夜思》之情节细化出来，因至繁文缛节。

望月之 20：Workings of My Mind in the Dark Silence of Night （心潮澎湃：在静深之夜）

读英文

In the dark silence of night.
每当夜深人静时。

The early light **whitened the window**.
一早的晨光照白了窗户。

A beam of moonlight illuminated a familiar-looking male and six others climbing the mountain behind them.
一束月光照亮了一个面熟的男人和六个紧随其后登山的人。

She **felt queer waking up** in the living-room.
在起居室醒来，我感到有点异样。

In **the quiet, secret night** she was by herself again.
安静而神秘的夜晚，她再次独自一人。

The silence in the room was deep as the night itself.
房间里的寂静，深如深夜。

Maureen **stretched back her neck towards the sky**, searching the dusk for the first sprinkle of stars.

莫琳沉思着，转回头，在薄暮里寻找今夜第一颗闪亮的星。

She stood **transfixed, lost in his meditations**.

她愣住了，站在那里，陷入了沉思。

Now that the deed was done, she **realized this with a wave of homesickness hard to dispel**.

现在木已成舟，她才清醒过来，感到心中有一种难以排遣的思家之痛。

The full moon's light was beginning to fade as it sank toward the west.

月亮西斜，满月渐亏。

英文散译

Workings of My Mind in the Dark Silence of Night

The window is whitened by a beam of frostlike moonlight, when I feel quite queer waking up by myself in the dark silence of the secret night. The silence in my bedroom is deep as the night itself. When I stretch my neck towards the sky, towards the moon which is bright and alone, I am transfixed, lost in my meditations, and there is a hurry, too, in all my thoughts, a turbulent, feverishly heated innermost workings of my mind — I realize this with a wave of homesickness hard to dispel. The full moon's light is beginning to fade as it sinks towards the west, but my fond memory of childhood home is not fading ….

英文诗译

Workings of My Mind in the Dark Silence of Night
Li Bai
The window is whitened by a beam of frostlike moonlight, when I feel
quite queer waking up by myself in the dark silence of the secret night.
The silence in my bedroom is deep as the night itself. When I
stretch my neck towards the sky, towards the moon which is
bright and alone, I am transfixed, lost in my meditations,
and there is a hurry, too, in all my thoughts, a turbulent,
feverishly heated innermost workings of my mind —
I realize this with a wave of homesickness hard

to dispel. The full moon's light is beginning

to fade as it sinks towards the west, but

my fond memory of child-

hood home is not

fading ....

回译

心潮澎湃：在静深之夜

一束霜一样的月光，刷白了窗户，神秘

之夜，我在黑暗的静寂之中醒来，感觉

异样。卧室里一片静寂，正如寂夜之

深。当我抬头望天，看向空中孤月，

我呆住了，陷入沉思；千愁万绪，

滚滚而来，我不禁心潮澎湃

——乡愁来袭，我感到

难以排遣。月亮西斜，

月光渐黯渐淡，而

我心中的童年家

乡的美好记忆，

却永不消

褪……

译人语

译诗标题 *Workings of My Mind in the Dark Silence of Night*，其中 workings，似乎不太容易理解，其实也最微妙，一般译者不会想到如此使用一个常见词语的。仔细品味如下英文句子中的 work 及其变异的使用：

... the innermost **workings** of this poor man's mind.

这个可怜的人心灵最深处的活动。

Her mind was **working** feverishly.

她脑海里思绪纷扰。

The warm dust **worked** on his heels like velvet, and melted the tension.

脚下温暖的灰尘像天鹅绒一样，融化了心中的紧张。

The depth of his emotion made him vulnerable and she had a feeling that somehow and at some time she so could **work** upon it as to induce him to forgive her.

他用情很深，使得他容易受到伤害。她有一种感觉，有朝一日，她总能设法利用这一点，劝诱他原谅自己。

I know how a bad guy's mind **works**—not that different from mine a while back.
我能猜着坏人的心思——和我原来的心思差不多。

There was a hurry, too, in all his thoughts, a turbulent and heated **working** of his heart, that contended against resignation. If, for a moment, he did feel resigned, then his wife and child who had to live after him, seemed to protest and to make it a selfish thing.

他感到千愁万绪滚滚而来，不禁心潮澎湃，心急如焚，无法做到听天安命。即使他确实平静了一会儿，在他死后还要活下去的妻儿却似乎又在抗议，把那平静叫作了自私。

最后一个例子中，不仅借用了 working，还借用了其句式，于是便有译文：there is a hurry, too, in all my thoughts, a turbulent, feverishly heated innermost workings of my mind。

望月之 21：Missing Helplessness in a Silent Night（静夜，思念流深）

读英文

The light from the window passed through the leaves of the tree outside, **sending shadows that rippled like water on the whitened wall**.

雨声停了，阳光穿过枝叶射进窗来，在白墙上映下流波一样的树影。

The summer light struck into the corner brilliantly **in the earlier part of the day**.

上午，太阳的光灿烂地照进这个街角。

He did not **lift his eyes** from his work.

目光没有从他的活计上移开。

The king then **lifted his eyes to Heaven**, and seeing the sun begin to fall low, he thus spoke.

这时，国王抬起头来注视天空，见太阳已经西沉，便说道。

He **spotted a thin ray of light** shining from between the shutters on the second floor.

从二楼的百叶窗之间，他发现了一条细细的光线。

A memory surged into his mind, one of those that Harold most feared.

哈罗德最恐惧的一段回忆又冒了出来。

I am longing to see her again.

我迫切希望再次见到她。

…and **the feeling of loneliness begins little by little to be less heavy on his heart**.

心上的孤独感也渐渐不再那么沉重。

… who **were very sorry for themselves this wet night**, I doubt not, and yearned for their country homes.

遇到这样潮湿的黑夜，他们一定觉得自己很可怜，而且很想念自己的家乡吧。

…but he **has no thoughts for** that.

但他根本没有想到这一点。

Hedgerows **reduced to** ditches, and drystone walls.

灌木丛逐渐消失，变成沟渠和干巴巴的石头墙。

And the laughter crashed out again, in wild paroxysms, the Professor's daughters **were reduced to shaking helplessness**.

人群中又爆发出一阵大笑，人们抽风般地笑着，教授的两个女儿笑得浑身打颤，要死要活的。

英文散译

Missing Helplessness in a Silent Night

My quiet, dark room is lit only by the moonlight pouring in through the window overhead, sending beams that gently ripple, in the latter part of the night, like water on the whitened frost-like floor. I lift my eyes to Heaven, and spot a moon, which is now full, quiet and mellow in the sky, before I lower my head in thought as a memory surges into my mind, a fond memory of my childhood home for which, sometime lost somewhere, I am longing …. When a feeling of loneliness, a feeling of homesickness, begins little by little to be heavier and heavier on my heart, I am very sorry for myself this very night. My thoughts throng for home, and I am reduced to missing helplessness ….

英文诗译

Missing Helplessness in a Silent Night

My quiet, dark room is lit only by the moonlight pouring in through the window overhead, sending beams that gently ripple, in the

latter part of the night, like water on the whitened frost-like

floor. I lift my eyes to Heaven, and spot a moon, which

is now full, quiet and mellow in the sky, before I lower

my head in thought as a memory surges into my

mind, a fond memory of my childhood home

for which, sometime lost somewhere, I am

longing …. When a feeling of loneliness,

a feeling of homesickness, begins little

by little to be heavier and heavier on

my heart, I am very sorry for myself

this very night. My thoughts throng

for home, and I am reduced

to missing helplessness ….

回译

静夜，思念流深

我静静的黑暗小屋，被头顶上方涌窗泄入的月光

点亮。后半夜，空中投下如水的光束，轻轻

荡漾，在如霜涂抹的地上。我抬头望天，

只见一轮明月，圆圆，静静，柔柔，

悬挂空中。我低头沉思，心中澎湃

着回忆，袅袅娜娜的童年家乡，

某时，某地，早已失去，我心

渴望……。一阵孤独之感，

一阵思乡之情，在我心头，

愈演愈烈；就这今晚，

在这静寂之夜，我，

自哀自怜。想家

之情，念家之思，

静夜流深，思

念流深……

译人语

英译中，my quiet, dark room is lit only by the moonlight pouring in through the window overhead, sending beams that gently ripple, in the latter part of the night, like water on the whitened frost-like floor. 除了上引的英文例子之外，还借鉴了如下英文句子：

Trees rose above and all around me in the quiet, dark room, lit only by the moonlight pouring in through the windows overhead.

英译中，I lift my eyes to Heaven, and spot a moon, which is now full, quiet and mellow in the sky, before I lower my head in thought as a memory surges into my mind, 还借鉴了霍克斯英译《红楼梦》第四回中的一个句子：

> 雨村低了头，半日说道："依你怎么着？"

Yu-cun lowered his head in thought. After a very long pause he asked, 'What do you think I ought to do?'

多处借鉴英文，译成一个句子，这样的句子，如果变通和衔接没有瑕疵，往往会成为很好的英文句子。有了很好的英文句子，即便不分行，也是很好的散文，具有浓浓诗意的散文。这样，往往比很多格律体译诗还要具有诗意。另外，借鉴名家名译中的英文，也是一个可行的方法。

望月之 22：Workings of My Mind in the Still Night（静夜，思如泉涌）

读英文

The carriage lamps **cast rays of light a little distance ahead of** them and she caught glimpses of the things they passed.

马车灯在她们前方投下几缕亮光，一路上她走马观花地看着路旁的事物。

A spotlight **hit** the stage.

一束聚光灯打在台上。

The **air** was **biting**, and **smelt of frost**.

空气冷得刺骨，霜气很重。

Holmes held up the paper so that **the sunlight shone full upon** it.

福尔摩斯把那张纸举起来，让阳光充分照亮它。

Just then **my eye was caught by** a small figure standing out in the sunlight amidst the rush of passers-by.

突然我看见外面太阳下来来往往的人群中站着一个小小的身影。

He went to one of the windows and threw open the shutter. **A flood of** warm **light streamed into** the **room**.

他走到一扇窗户前拉起了百叶窗，一大片阳光流泻到屋里来。

Lying in the bed with the **moonlight streaming** dimly over her, she pictured the whole scene in her mind.

躺在床上，她全身沐浴着朦胧的月光，心里揣摩着通盘的情景。

Before my taxi had covered a mile, **my thoughts had drifted to** the work I intended to do that day.

出租车开出去不到一里地，我就想起当天要做的工作。

The days were shortening now and the mellow light of the evening was **agreeable and a little melancholy**.

此时的天也越来越短，傍晚柔和的暮色惬意宜人，还带有一点点伤感忧郁。

He had no idea that this could **dwell in the thoughts of** his fair young wife.
他可没料到这话会在他年轻美丽的妻子的脑海中徘徊。

The night deepened.
夜色渐浓。

英文散译

Workings of My Mind in the Still Night

The moon casts rays of light a little distance ahead of my bed, beams of light hitting the ground, which awakens me from my sound sleep. The air is biting, and smells of frost. Now the moonlight shines full upon my face, and my eye is caught by the brilliance of the moon, from which a flood of cold light keeps streaming into my room as my mind drifts back to my hometown. I seem to catch glimpses of the mellow light of my childhood moon, suggestive of my hometown, my villagers, my neighbors, my sisters and brothers, and my parents .... The moonscape, agreeable and a little melancholy, reduces me to nostalgia, which dwells in my thoughts. The night, the still night, is still deepening ... the innermost workings of my mind are also deepening ....

英文诗译

Workings of My Mind in the Still Night

The moon casts rays of light a little distance ahead of my bed, beams of light hitting the ground, which awakens me from my sound sleep. The air is biting, and smells of frost. Now the moonlight shines full upon my face, and my eye is caught by the brilliance of the moon,

from which a flood of cold light keeps streaming into my room

as my mind drifts back to my hometown. I seem to catch

glimpses of the mellow light of my childhood moon,

suggestive of my hometown, my villagers, my

neighbors, my sisters and brothers, and my

parents .... The moonscape, agreeable

and a little melancholy, reduces me

to nostalgia, which dwells in my

thoughts. The night, the still

night, is still deepening ...

the innermost workings

of my mind are also

deepening ....

回译

静夜，思如泉涌
月光在我床前投下几缕亮光，落地有声，
把我从梦中惊醒：空气冷得刺骨，
霜气凝重。月光朗照脸上——
眼见月之灼灼，冷光如潮，灌注
屋内，此时，我魂归故里。我
仿佛看见了童年月亮的柔光，
联翩浮想于我的家乡，我的
村庄，我的邻居街坊，我的
兄弟姐妹，我的亲父亲娘
……月色惬意可人，却
糅合一丝忧郁之光，我
不免感伤——乡愁，
在我思想深处定居。
夜，宁静之夜，静

夜流深……在我

心灵深处，愁

绪深涌……

译人语

"望月之 20"标题的英译，就用了 workings，此译标题的英译也用了这个单词，且诗内再用：the innermost workings of my mind are also deepening。除了"望月之 20"中 workings 相关的英文例子之外，可参看另外一例：

He once said, "I must have two girls to do my lessons with me if I am to remember the words and understand the sense. Otherwise my mind will simply not work. "

他说："必得两个女儿陪着我读书，我方能认得字，心上也明白，不然我心里自己糊涂。"

如此简单的一个 work，及其变形 workings，却能用得如此令人回味，可见文字艺术之妙。

另外，"月光……落地有声"，"乡愁，在我思想深处定居"，"夜，宁静之夜，静夜流深……"等，如此译文，明显带有了现代诗的味道。经典咏流传，正需古诗英译的现代化。

望月之 23：Homesickness in the Depth of Night（静夜思乡）

读英文

But she was awakened by a loud knocking. At first, since it was interwoven with the dream from which she was aroused, she could not **attach the sound to reality**.

她被一阵闹哄哄的敲门声惊醒了。开始她还以为是在做梦，没有意识到敲门声是真的。

He **lifted his head** from the pages flapping in the breeze.
他抬起头来，书页在风中翻动着。

His stony eyes **bore into** mine.
他冷漠的目光似乎钻入了我。

His blue eyes seemed to **bore into** her.
他的一双蓝眼睛似乎要穿透她。

Then he **lowered himself** into the leather sofa.
然后他弯下身来，坐到皮沙发上。

Did he **ache for** her, the way I **ached for** the mother I had never met?
他想念她吗，就像我想念一直没能见面的妈妈一样？

英文散译

Homesickness in the Depth of Night

I am awakened by a beam of flickering moonlight through the window panes and, since it is interwoven with the dream from which I am aroused, I cannot attach it to reality. I lift my head from the pillow, to see a silvery moon, which seems to bore into me, before lowering myself, to find the frost-like floor, and I begin to ache for home.

英文诗译

Homesickness in the Depth of Night

I am awakened by a beam of flickering moonlight
through the window panes and, since it is interwoven with the dream from which I am
aroused, I cannot attach it to reality.
I lift my head from the pillow, to
see a silvery moon, which seems
to bore into me, before lowering
myself, to find the frost-
like floor, and I
begin to ache
for home.

回译

静夜思乡
一束闪烁的月光，穿透窗户
格子，把我惊醒：月光
交织夜梦，亦真，
亦幻。我欠身
抬头，见一轮
银月，其光如针，
欲穿透我；
躬身垂目，
见地面如霜，
回家的渴望——
油然而生。

译人语

从英文散译来看，译文用了两个句号，也就是两个句子。连词 and，关系代词 from which 和 which，不定式符号 to，介词 before 等，都是地道的英文衔接手段，通过这些，句子显得复杂化了。而相应的汉语回译，又走向了相对的语言简约。汉英语言的不同特征，于此显然可见。译诗整体看来并不复杂，却也具有一些现代诗的特征。

望月之 24：Flight of Thought in the Depth of Night（深夜：思绪飘逸）

读英文

She became distantly aware that the light had grown strangely brighter and was **flickering** gently.

她模糊地意识到光线奇怪地变得明亮起来，轻轻摇曳着。

The fields **look frosty** this morning.

今晨的田野看起来有霜冻。

Fleur was wearing a very simple white dress and seemed to be emitting a strong, **silvery glow**.

芙蓉穿着一件非常简单的白色连衣裙，周身似乎散发出一种强烈的银光。

Jean can **conjure up** a good meal in half an hour.

琼能在半小时内变戏法似地做出一顿美味的饭菜。

Thirteen years ago she found herself having to **conjure** a career from thin air.

十三年前她认识到自己得白手起家闯出一番事业来。

The term 'school culture' can **conjure memories of** one's own schooling, **imbued with fond nostalgia** for some and quite the opposite for others.

"学校文化"一词令人想起上学的情景，带着美好的回忆，夹杂着酸楚的滋味。

He **was imbued with** a desire for social justice.

他满怀着寻求社会正义的愿望。

Once again I **am overcome by** the feeling that we have lost such a good comrade.

我们失去了这样一位好同志，想到这，我再次感到很难受。

And yet, **she was overcome by the nostalgia.**

可她还是被对这里的眷恋之情所攫取。

英文散译

Flight of Thought in the Depth of Night

The moonlight is flickering through the window panes, and the floor looks frosty. The silvery glow of the bright moon conjures memories of my home, imbued with fond nostalgia, by which I am overcome.

英文诗译

Flight of Thought in the Depth of Night

The moonlight is flickering through

the window panes, and the floor

looks frosty. The silvery glow

of the bright moon conjures

memories of my home,

imbued with fond

nostalgia, by

which I am

overcome.

回译

深夜：思绪飘逸

月光闪闪烁烁穿过

窗格，屋内地面

如霜。月亮的

银光唤醒家

乡之记忆，

带着甜蜜
的乡愁，
情不能
已。

译人语

此译虽然简单，却不乏诗意，尤其是 conjures memories 和 I am overcome by fond nostalgia 等，从英语借鉴而来，深有余味。即便散文读之，也是耐人寻味的句子了。

望月之 25：Deep Night Thinking （深夜的思念）

读英文

It was **brilliant moonlight**, and the **soft effect** of the light over the sea and sky — merged together in one great, silent mystery — was beautiful beyond words.

天上有一轮明月，柔和的月光洒在天空中，流泻于海上。这种巨大而寂静的神秘力量将天地之间融合在了一起，此等美景真是难以用笔墨来形容。

The room was **thickly carpeted**.

房间铺着厚厚的地毯。

There is **a gleam of light**; I can **feel the air blowing upon me**.

有一束光，我能感觉到微风吹在我身上。

He **glanced up** in surprise.

看到她，他吃了一惊。

She stood looking at him **in gloomy, heavy silence, for some time**.

她沉郁、默默地看了他一会儿。

Birkin, looking at them, **felt a pain of tenderness for** them.

伯金看着他们两个人，感到很心疼他们。

But he **felt something icy gathering at his heart**.

可是他感到心头愈来愈发凉。

And the laughter crashed out again, in wild paroxysms, the Professor's daughters **were reduced to** shaking helplessness.

人群中又爆发出一阵大笑，人们抽风般地笑着，教授的两个女儿笑得浑身打颤，要死要活的。

She was in **some self-satisfied world of her own**.
她有自己的世界，很惬意。

英文散译

Deep Night Thinking

A beam of brilliant moonlight through the window brings a soft effect upon the ground: thinly carpeted with frost. In the gleam of light, I can feel the gentle air of my native land blowing upon me. I glance up at the silvery moon in gloomy, heavy silence, for a great while, before I feel a pain of tenderness for my home, something sweet gathering at my heart, and I am reduced to some self-satisfied world of my own.

英文诗译

Deep Night Thinking

A beam of brilliant moonlight through the window

brings a soft effect upon the ground: thinly

carpeted with frost. In the gleam of light,

I can feel the gentle air of my native

land blowing upon me. I glance up

at the moon in gloomy, heavy

silence, for some time, before

I feel a pain of tenderness for

my home, something sweet

gathering at my heart,

and I am reduced to

some self-satisfied

world of my

own.

回译

> 深夜的思念
> 一束明亮的月光，透过窗户，
> 柔和于地上：薄薄的一层
> 冷霜。银光晃动，感到
> 故乡的微风，吹拂在
> 我身上。举目望月，
> 沉郁、静默多时，
> 顿觉一丝柔情，
> 疼痛来袭，甜
> 蜜聚涌，我
> 心归故里：
> 自足、自
> 闭、自
> 惬意
>
> 。

译人语

译文之借用，常有妙处，如 a soft effect upon the ground；in gloomy, heavy silence；a pain of tenderness for my home；something sweet gathering at my heart；some self-satisfied world of my own，或者直接借鉴自英文，或者稍作改动，语言质量得以提升。回译的结尾处，"自足、自闭、自惬意。"措词具有同源修辞格的美学效果。另外，用句号收束译诗，独立成行，罕见而新颖。

望月之 26：Deep Thinking in the Depth of Night（静夜静思）

读英文

She realized that **it was faintly moonlight**.

她知道那是淡淡的月光。

Suddenly he **looked full at** her.

突然，他的眼睛直视着她。

She turned and **looked full** in his eyes.

她转过身，凝视着他的眼。

She **looked at him with lingering**, friendly **eyes**.

她的眼睛望着沃丁顿，目光友善，久未移开。

Martha looked **reflective** again.

玛莎看上去又若有所思了。

Waddington **looked at her reflectively**. Her abstracted **gaze rested on** the smoothness of the river.

沃丁顿若有所思地望着她。只见她那漫不经心的目光落到了平静的河面上。

She looked at him again. Tears sprang into her eyes once more and **her heart was very full**.

她又看了他一眼，泪水再一次从眼里涌了出来，她的心里满满的，百味杂陈。

A heavy cruelty **welled up in her**.

她的心变残酷了。

英文散译

Deep Thinking in the Depth of Night

Faint moonlight glimmers before my bed, suggestive of frost aground. I look up full at the moon lingeringly, reflectively, my gaze resting on it, and my heart is very full, when homesickness is welling up in me.

英文诗译

Deep Thinking in the Depth of Night

Faint moonlight glimmers before my

bed, suggestive of frost aground.

I look up full at the moon linger-

ingly, reflectively, my gaze

resting on it, and my heart

is very full, when home-

sickness is

welling

up in

me.

回译

静夜静思

淡淡的月光，床前闪烁，

似乎是地上之霜。我

盯着月亮，恋恋

不舍，若有所思，

目光融于月光，

内心无比充盈

——乡愁，

自内心

升起

。

译人语

英文句子 She looked at him with lingering, friendly eyes 中，lingering 用作形容词，译诗变成副词 lingeringly，与 reflectively 并置，不仅表意好，而且造成单词尾韵。回译中，英文 my gaze resting on it，对应"目光融于月光"，貌离，而神合。从句 when homesickness is welling up in me，对应"——乡愁，自内心升起。"显然，when 被翻译成了破折号，可谓巧妙。最后，又以句号单独成行，结束译诗，可谓诗终，而意，犹未尽也。

望月之 27：Quiet Night Homesickness（静夜乡思）

读英文

The garden **is bright with** flowers.
鲜花满园。

We must **trace the source of** these noxious gases.
我们必须查出毒气的来源。

If you **trace the source of** the mind, you find it is nothingness.
如果你追踪心的源头，你发现它什么都不是。

His glaring eyes are **looking** straight **upward**.
他怒视的双眼直向上看。

His reply **reduced me to silence**.
他的回答使我哑口无言。

You almost **reduce me to tears**.
你快要让我流下眼泪来了。

英文散译

Quiet Night Homesickness

The ground before my bed is bright with light, which seems like hoar frost. I trace the source of light by upward looking, to find a wheel of moon, which reduces me to homesickness, in this quiet night.

英文诗译

Quiet Night Homesickness

The ground before my bed is bright
with light, which seems like hoar
frost. I trace the source of light
by upward looking, to find
a wheel of moon, which
reduces me to home-
sickness, in
this quiet
night.

回译

静夜乡思

床前的地上，有光，
而亮；看起来，像
霜。追光，求源，
抬头张望，只见
圆月一轮，引我
思乡——就在
这宁静
的晚
上。

译人语

英译的亮点，该是 I trace the source of light by upward looking，描写形象生动，通过想象，再现了诗人思乡的一些细节。整首译诗干净利索，力图烘托思乡的意境。回译之佳，在于标点的添加运用，尤其逗号，最后的破折号也好。这些标点的使用，延缓了读者的阅读体验，暗示了诗人思乡之漫长与深幽。

望月之 28：Contemplative Sadness in the Dead of Night（深夜：忧郁而沉思）

读英文

He sat **with contemplative sadness** on the hearth.
他有点忧郁地坐蹲在炉前地毯上似乎沉思着。

It was **in the dead of night**.
夜深了。

The sight inspired him with nostalgia.
这景象激起了他的怀旧之情。

But it did not pass, and **a crisis gained upon him.**
可这绝境并未过去，危机渐渐向他袭来。

The next day however, **he felt wistful and yearning**.
可到了第二天，他感到一阵阵的渴求欲。

Then **a hot passion of tenderness for her filled his heart**.
随后他心中升起一股对她的温柔激情。

英文散译

Contemplative Sadness in the Dead of Night

The floor before my bed is frosty with a beam of faint moonlight through the window in the dead of night. The sight inspires me with nostalgia, which is gaining upon me: wistful and yearning, I straighten up with contemplative sadness, when a hot passion of tenderness for my home is filling my heart.

英文诗译

Contemplative Sadness in the Dead of Night
The floor before my bed is frosty with a beam
of faint moonlight through the window in
the dead of night. The sight inspires me
with nostalgia, which is gaining upon
me: wistful and yearning, I straighten
up with contemplative sadness,
when a hot passion
of tenderness for
my home is
filling my
heart.

回译

深夜：忧郁而沉思
深夜，一束淡淡的月光，透窗
而入，照在床前如霜的地上。
此景，激起了我内心的思
乡之情，浸袭而来，不能
自己：渴着，求着，思着，
念着……我挺直腰身，
负荷着忧郁与沉思，
心中，一股思念
家乡的温柔
激情，涌
着，荡
着……

译人语

英译中，the sight inspires me with nostalgia, which is gaining upon me: wistful and yearning, I straighten up with contemplative sadness, when a hot passion of tenderness for my home is filling my heart，读来就像是英文作家笔下的英文——其实，不正是的吗？因为我们把英文作家笔下的多个句子糅合了起来，自然英文气息浓郁。同译中，又发挥了汉语的优势，如"渴着，求着，思着，念着……涌着，荡着……"，不仅强调了内心动态的进行时，而且行文的节奏，也为之铿然。"负荷着忧郁与沉思"，有了汉语新诗的意味。整体看来，较之英文，回译多出一行，不拘泥于英文之文字与行数，意在带来回译之后汉语新诗的诗味。

望月之 29：Moony and Dreamy in a Soft, Still Night（静谧之夜：月光与梦乡）

读英文

It takes him a long time **to wake from his night's sleep**.
他过了很久才从睡梦中醒来。

I walked slowly along the passage to the door by the archway, my mind still blunt and slow as though **I had just woken from a long sleep**.
我拖着缓慢的步子朝拱形市道旁的门户走去。思想依然迟钝麻木，好比刚从一夜酣睡中苏醒过来。

It was **a sunny, soft morning**，and he lingered in the garden paths, looking at the flowers that had come out during his absence.
那天早晨阳光和煦，他流连在花园小径上，观赏着他离家后盛开的鲜花。

And gradually **a feeling of sorrow came over her**.
渐渐地，她开始感到哀伤。

Walter **looked at his guest with a cold and ironic gaze**.
瓦尔特凝视着他的客人，目光冷冰冰的，带着嘲讽。

He **gradually gathered the whole situation into his mind**.
他对矿区的全部局势胸有成竹了。

Her father looked at her, and **his heart ran hot with tenderness, an anguish of poignant love**.

父亲看着她，心中洋溢着一股温情，父爱流深。

英文散译

Moony and Dreamy in a Soft, Still Night

Waking from a sleep in a soft, still night, I find it moony, dreamy, the ground silvery with frosty faint light. A feeling of sorrow comes over me, as I lift my eyes to look at the moon with a wistful, thoughtful gaze, gradually gathering my hometown into my mind, and my heart runs hot with tenderness, an anguish of poignant love.

英文诗译

Moony and Dreamy in a Soft, Still Night

Waking from a sleep in a soft, still night,
I find it moony, dreamy, the ground
silvery with frosty faint light. A
feeling of sorrow comes over
me, as I lift my eyes to look
at the moon with a wistful,
thoughtful gaze, gradually
gathering my hometown
into my mind, and my
heart runs hot with
tenderness, an
anguish of
poignant
love.

回译

静谧之夜：月光与梦乡
静谧之夜，我从梦中醒来，

月光——依然如梦；床前，

月光银白，冷淡如霜。

抬头，望见一轮月亮，

目光凝思、感伤，

我开始感到一阵

悲凉；慢慢，慢

慢地，故乡在

我心中成形，

于是，我心，

一股股温情

溢洋，痛

着，爱

着……

译人语

英译中，有不少内韵之使用，例如 sleep, soft, still；frosty, faint；gradually, gathering，分别形成三组头韵；moony 与 dreamy，wistful 与 thoughtful，分别押单词尾韵。

译诗中，gathering my hometown into my mind，借鉴自如下句子：He gradually gathered the whole situation into his mind（他对矿区的全部局势胸有成竹了），这个相对不容易理解，其实最为巧妙。对应回译："故乡在我心中成形"，也只是大概的翻译而已，其中意味，不可尽传。随后的英译：my heart runs hot with tenderness, an anguish of poignant love，对应回译："我心，一股股温情溢洋，痛着，爱着……"。情感大体对应，文字却有变化。措词运字，中文英文有时截然不同，貌离神合之处，最得翻译之妙。

望月之 30：Moonlit Night: Eagerness to Be Home（月夜：想家情急）

读英文

That is an **illusion** of yours.
那是你瞎想。

Trace a rumor to its source.
追查谣言的根源。

She **gave him a long look** with those beautiful eyes of hers and tried to smile.
她用自己那双美丽的眼睛凝视着他。她试图微笑一下。

She **looked back at him as if full of gratitude**.
她回头看他，目光似含感激。

She **peers through the mist**, trying to find the right path.
她透过雾眯着眼看，想找出正确的路。

We **are on fire with anxiety and eagerness**.
我们充满了忧虑和急切。

英文散译

Moonlit Night: Eagerness to Be Home

A beam of light before my bed, illusively suggestive of frost on the ground.
Tracing the light to its source, I find the moon, which I give a long look as if full of

yearning and, peering through the mist, I seem to be on fire with eagerness to be home.

英文诗译

Moonlit Night: Eagerness to Be Home
Li Bai
A beam of light before my bed, illusively
suggestive of frost on the ground.
Tracing the light to its source,
I find the moon, which I give
a long look as if full of
yearning and, peering
through the mist, I
seem to be on fire
with eagerness
to be home.

回译

月夜：想家情急
床前，一束亮光，梦幻似的，
令人想起大地之霜。追光
求源，我发现了月亮，
久久凝视着，充满
着渴望。透过迷
雾，我急切切，
急切切地
渴望着
归乡
。

译人语

借鉴英文之时，有时几乎直接拿来，有时却需要变通，甚至比较大的变通。

例如英文句子：That is an illusion of yours（那是你瞎想），句中名词 illusion，译文却变通使用了跟 illusion 同源的副词 illusively：illusively suggestive of frost on the ground，这就需要译者的语言变通能力。同样，从英译到汉语的回译，也多有变通。例如：I seem to be on fire with eagerness to be home，回译："我急切切，急切切地渴望着归乡。"翻译，必须灵活才好，无论从古典汉诗译成英文，还是从英语译文回译成汉语，都是一样道理。

望月之 31：Still Night: Wistful Reminiscences（宁静的夜晚，怅惘的回忆）

读英文

Such **wishful thinking** of theirs will never be realized.
他们的这种痴心妄想是永远也不会实现的。

Let's not waste a precious second on **wishful thinking** or useless regrets. Life really is too short.
我们不要将宝贵的时间浪费在痴心妄想或作无谓的惋惜上，生命实在是太短暂了。

The boy **looks with wistful eyes at** the toy on display.
那男孩看著展出的玩具，眼中流露出渴望的神情。

She **looked at him with a long, slow inscrutable look**, as he stood before her negligently, the water standing in beads all over his skin.
戈珍缓缓地把目光投向他，眼神怪异地看着他。他大大咧咧地站在她面前，皮肤上泛着水珠。

The poor mother **has wistful reminiscences of** her lost youth.
这个贫穷的母亲怅惘地回忆她已经逝去的青春。

She **lay there inert**, I thought she must be dead.

她躺在那儿一动不动，我想她一定是死了。

But he did not move, **for a long time he remained inert, his head dropped on his breast**.

可他没有动，垂着头一动不动地坐了好久。

英文散译

Still Night: Wistful Reminiscences

A splash of light before my bed — hoarfrost on the ground? Looking up with wishful eyes at the moon, a long, slow look, I have wistful reminiscences of my hometown and, for a long time I remain inert, my head dropping on my breast.

英文诗译

Still Night: Wistful Reminiscences

A splash of light before my bed — hoarfrost

on the ground? Looking up with wishful

eyes at the moon, a long, slow look,

I have wistful reminiscences of

my hometown and, for a long

time I remain inert, my head

dropping on my

breast.

回译

宁静的夜晚，怅惘的回忆

床前洒落着一片月光——地上之霜？

抬头，瞥见月亮，渴望的目光，

长久而缓慢，不禁回忆起

我的故乡，内心充满

怅惘，时间似乎

凝固，我一动

不动，垂头，

感伤……

译人语

在 a splash of light 中，splash 虽为名词，却动词含义十分明显，回译"洒落"，恰好。接着，— hoarfrost on the ground? 破折号带起疑问句，描写心理活动，自然而顺畅。从音韵角度而言，before 与 bed 押头韵，又与 hoarfrost 押元音韵；with 与 wishful 押头韵；long，slow，look 押头韵，因 slow 的开音轻读，头韵效果明显。另外，译诗中的两个单词：wistful（渴望的；忧思的；留恋的）与 wishful（怀有希望的；表达愿望的）相近而区别，单词头韵兼尾韵。这些，都是英诗押韵之本色，不同于汉诗单一的诗行尾韵，译者读者，于此不可不察。

望月之 32：Midnight: Something Lost Somewhere（午夜：若有所失）

读英文

A wedge of moonlight streamed in through the window.
一束楔子形的月光，透过窗户流泻进来。

A spotlight **hit** the stage.
一束聚光灯打在台上。

The beauty of the scene may have been enhanced to our eyes by the fact that we had just come together after a night of some anxiety.
经过昨晚的风波，入眼的美景更平添了许多秀色。

He **lifted his head** from the pages flapping in the breeze.
他抬起头来，书页在风中翕动。

Then **he lowered himself into** the leather sofa.
他弯身坐在皮沙发上。

Did he **ache for** her, the way I **ached fo**r the mother I had never met?
他想念她吗？就像我想念我从未见过面的母亲一样。

The Might-have-been shivered and vanished, **dim as a dream,** into the waste realms of non-existence.
这些可能性一闪即逝，如梦境般模糊不清，终究化为乌有。

英文散译

Midnight: Something Lost Somewhere

Midnight sees a wedge of moonlight streaming in through the window, before hitting the ground in front of my bed. The beauty of the scene, suggestive of frost, has been enhanced to my eyes by the fact that I lift my head to gaze at the moon before lowering myself into nostalgia where I ache for my home, dim as a dream and distant as heaven ....

英文诗译

Midnight: Something Lost Somewhere

Midnight sees a wedge of moonlight streaming in
through the window, before hitting the ground
in front of my bed. The beauty of the scene,
suggestive of frost, has been enhanced
to my eyes by the fact that I lift
my head to gaze at the moon
before lowering myself into
nostalgia where I ache
for my home, dim as
a dream and
distant as
heaven
....

回译

午夜：若有所失
午夜，一束楔子形的月光，透过
窗户，流泻进来，打在我床前
的地上。如霜的美景，入眼，
愈秀——抬头望天，只见
皎皎空中，孤月一轮；

内心，瞬间塌陷于

乡愁。我禁不住

思念家乡，梦

境般模糊，

天堂般

遥

远

……

译人语

诗题译作：《午夜：若有所失》，似乎离《静夜思》有些距离。然而，当我们想起袅袅娜娜的故乡之时，难道有时不正是这样的心态的吗？人，不能两次踏进同一条河流；人，不能两次踏进自己的故乡。情至深处，故乡之情，故乡之思，可以堪哉？译文结语："梦境般模糊，天堂般遥远……"，与诗题呼应。如果说译诗多了点细节的呈现，也只是译者的人生体悟而已。思李白之所思，想李白之所想。作李氏太白静夜之思，译文方能入情。

望月之 33：Thoughts Racing Through the Sleepy Stillness of the Midnight （想家的念头，闪过午夜的沉寂）

读英文

All kinds of thoughts **raced through** my mind.
各种各样的想法闪过我的脑海。

Only the whisper of the redescending birds and the thunder of the distant waves broke in upon **the sleepy stillness of the afternoon**.
只有鸟的降落声和远处的浪击声，打破了午后的沉寂。

The abyssal **depths** of the ocean.
海洋深渊。

Music of great emotional **depth**.
饱含深情的音乐。

Never did the moon **rise with a milder radiance** over great London.
升起的月亮以从未如此温柔地光照在伟大的伦敦城。

I was standing, **rapt in the peaceful beauty of the scene**, when I was aware that something was moving under the shadow of the copper beeches.
我站在那里，沉浸在美丽宁静的夜色中，忽然间察觉有什么东西在紫铜榉树丛阴影下移动。

My thoughts turned to home.
我的思绪转到了家里。

英文散译

Thoughts Racing Through the Sleepy Stillness of the Midnight

The depth of the night is enhanced by the light of the moon, which is rising with a mild radiance in the boundless sky, breaking in upon the sleepy stillness of the midnight. The silvery window frames such a scene, in whose peaceful beauty I am rapt, all kinds of thoughts racing through my mind, turning to home ….

英文诗译

Thoughts Racing Through the Sleepy Stillness of the Midnight

The depth of the night is enhanced by the light of the moon,

which is rising with a mild radiance in the boundless

sky, breaking in upon the sleepy stillness of

the midnight. The silvery window frames

such a scene, in whose peaceful beauty

I am rapt, all kinds of thoughts

racing through my mind,

turning to home ….

回译

想家的念头，闪过午夜的沉寂

月光朗照，深夜愈深；无垠之夜空，

月亮缓升，遍洒温柔之光，惊了

午夜的沉寂。银白的窗户，定格

渺然之美景——如此静美，

陶醉我心。想家的念头，

闪过我的脑海，思绪

奔涌，向往着

家乡……

译人语

诗题《想家的念头，闪过午夜的沉寂》，似乎正是《静夜思》的当代阐释和演绎，从唐代的李白，走向了当下的新诗。如果不是来自英文阅读的灵感，该不会想起这么一个诗歌标题的。整首译诗，似乎有些偏离原诗，如"床前"、"疑是地上霜"、"举头望"、"低头"等，均未译出，不见痕迹；整首诗 20 个字，竟然 12 个未译。然而，译诗却对夜空之明月，以及内心之乡思，进行特写镜头式的详描细绘。其实，《静夜思》之关键字，应该两个：一"月"，一"思"。望月而思乡，乃《静夜思》之灵魂。而只要诗的灵魂译出，其它细节，在译文中，可能就会成为逸出的枝节，无关乎大雅。

望月之 34：*Still Night: Sudden Homesickness*（宁静之夜：思乡心切）

读英文

Where can one get a **peep** at her?

在什么地方可以见到她呢?

We had to walk past quietly, talking in whispers, and dared not even take a **peep** inside.

我们要轻轻地走过，低声地说话，也不敢往屋里窥视。

I was **awakened** next morning **by** the sound of voices.

第二天早晨，我被声音惊醒了。

Without **lifting her eyes** from the page she replied …

她不把眼睛从书上抬起，回答他。

As he combed his gingery brown hair, he noticed **with sudden homesickness** that it was the same color as his good old shell.

梳理着姜黄色的头发，他突然意识到这正是他从前那个玳瑁梳子的颜色，于是乡愁袭来。

She spent an hour in **quiet contemplation**.

她静静地沉思了一个小时。

英文散译

Still Night: Sudden Homesickness

A silvery beam of moonlight keeps peeping through the window, onto the ground in front of my bed, by which I am awakened. I trace the source of the frosty air by lifting my eyes heavenward, to get a glimpse of the brilliant moon with sudden homesickness, plunging me into the depths of quiet contemplation ….

英文诗译

Still Night: Sudden Homesickness
A silvery beam of moonlight keeps peeping through
the window, onto the ground in front of my bed,
by which I am awakened. I trace the source
of the frosty air by lifting my eyes heavenward, to get a glimpse of the brilliant
moon with sudden homesickness,
plunging me into the depths of
quiet contemplation ….

回译

宁静之夜：思乡心切
一束银白的月光，透过窗户，流泻
入室，洒落在我床前的地上——
我被惊醒。空气如霜，我追根
求源，仰头望，只见空中
明月高悬——乡愁来袭，
我瞬间沦陷：陷入了
静思，沉入了
默想。

译人语

译文中，a silvery beam of moonlight keeps peeping through the window，其中，peep 是动词，而"读英文"的两个英文句子中，peep 却是名词。其实，get a peep 也好，take a peep 也罢，peep 虽为名词，却动词意义十分明显。另外，I trace the source of the frosty air by ….，借鉴自这样一个英文句子：Trace a rumor to its source（追查谣言的根源）。因为此句之前使用过，便不在"读英

文"中列出。除了英文借用之外，介词 through 和 onto 的并列，by which 的使用，使译文具有了浓郁的英文味道；而 plunging me into the depths of，则加强了诗的语气，深化了诗的意境。

望月之 35：Spell of the Midnight Moon（魅：午夜之月）

读英文

I have never seen such **spellbinding** flowers in the park.

公园里的鲜花从未令我如此心醉神迷过。

Delay **spells** losses.

拖延招致损失。

By staying out, it would seem the night was not yet over. Returning would only **spell** the end of it.

不回去，觉得这夜还没有完，一回去，这夜就算完了。

Entranced, he was silent for a long space, **spellbound**.

他入迷了，着魔了，沉默了很长一段时间。

His audience had listened like children, **spellbound** by his words.

他的观众像孩子般倾听着，对他的话十分着迷。

We had to carry the piano up three **flights** of stairs.

我们不得不抬着钢琴上了三段楼梯。

英文散译

Spell of the Midnight Moon

The floor in front of my bed is frosty with a beam of light from the moon, the midnight moon which is spellbinding. The scene spells homesickness for me, and I am spellbound with a boundless flight of thoughts, which are carrying me heavenward, homeward ….

英文诗译

Spell of the Midnight Moon
The floor in front of my bed is frosty with a beam
of light from the moon, the midnight moon
which is spellbinding. The scene spells
homesickness for me, and I am
spellbound with a boundless
flight of thoughts, which
are carrying me
heavenward,
homeward
….

回译

魅：午夜之月
床前地上，被月光照亮，
如银似霜；午夜之月，
令人心醉神迷。面对
此景，我不禁开始
思乡，着了魔
一样，思想飘
逸着，带我，
向着天堂，
向着家乡
……。

译人语

美国作家 Peter Steinhart 曾写过一篇 *Spell of the Rising Moon*（《月升之魅》）

的散文，由此想到了《静夜思》的题目：*Spell of the Midnight Moon*，可谓巧妙，这里的 spell，意为"咒语；魔力"。随后，译文使用了另外三个 spell 的同源词：spellbinding（引人入胜的），spells（意味着）和 spellbound（出神的；被迷住的），从而带来译文的耐品耐味。另外，floor，front，frosty，from；bed，beam；moon，midnight；scene，spells；with，which 等，分别押头韵；spellbound 与 boundless 押元音韵；heavenward 与 homeward 押头韵兼尾韵。因此，译诗无韵而铿锵，一气而流泻。

望月之 36：Deep Night: a Mosaic of Memories（静夜：斑驳的回忆）

读英文

A mosaic of fields, rivers and woods lay below us.
我们下方是由田野、河流和林木交织成的图画。

Living under the skies, the forest is for me a temple, a cathedral made of tree canopies and **dancing light**, especially when it is raining and quiet.
对我来说，生长在蓝天下的丛林就象一座庙宇，一个用树冠和跳动的光线组成的大教堂，特别是在下雨和宁静中。

And the benefits **spill into** one of Spain's poorest regions.
而邻近的西班牙最贫困的地区也从中受益不浅。

Everything was covered in **a film of** dust.
所有的东西都蒙上了一层灰尘。

He **is entranced by** the kindness of her smile.
她善意的微笑令他着迷。

"I just thought you should know," he says, and turns **to slump back** toward the house.
"我只是觉得你应该知道一下"，他说完就向房子走去。

The photos are grainy, **blotchy and blurry**.
这些照片图像斑驳，而且模糊。

英文散译

Deep Night: a Mosaic of Memories

Awake, I find myself lying on an unfamiliar bed, when the dancing moonlight spills into my room and scatters across the floor, suggestive of a film of frost. Gazing out the window, I am entranced by the splendor of the moon and, as my head slumps back, I see a wheel, a bright wheel of moon — it is so wistful and beautiful, this familiar moon, this familiar moonlight, for which I am already feeling some nostalgia. And my thoughts turn to home, bringing to mind a mosaic of memories — a touch of homesickness lingers and swells in the tides of my heart, so much so that my eyes are blotchy and blurry, through the silvery light of the moon.

英文诗译

Deep Night: a Mosaic of Memories

Awake, I find myself lying on an unfamiliar bed, when the dancing
moonlight spills into my room and scatters across the floor,
suggestive of a film of frost. Gazing out the window, I am
entranced by the splendor of the moon and, as my head
slumps back, I see a wheel, a bright wheel of moon —
it is so wistful and beautiful, this familiar moon, this
familiar moonlight, for which I am already feeling
some nostalgia. And my thoughts turn to home,
bringing to mind a mosaic of memories —
a touch of homesickness lingers and swells
in the tides of my heart, so much so that
my eyes are blotchy and blurry,
through the silvery
light of the
moon.

回译

静夜：斑驳的回忆
醒来，我发现自己躺在一张陌生的床上，

舞动的月光溢入我的房间，遍洒地板，
好像一层薄薄的冷霜。望向窗外，
月之光华令人入迷；回头侧卧，
我看见一轮明月，其光璨璨
　　——若美若思；这熟悉的月
亮，这熟悉的月光，乡愁，
不觉而生。吾心归乡里，
心中塞满斑驳的回忆
　　——乡愁逗留，随
心潮而澎湃；我
泪眼模糊，迷
离于银色的
月光之
中。

译人语

　　静夜，见月而思念故乡，尤其念起时隔多年的童年的故乡，内心的回忆，白是斑而驳之，模而糊之。陌生的床上——客居他乡也。"客"，乃是中国古典诗词中一个常见的名词，为西方文化所缺失。英译若作 guest，显然错误；traveler，只是旅游者；roamer 或 wanderer，较好，因有漂泊云游之意，仿佛沾边。李白之"低头思故乡"，含人生多少惨痛体验。译文注入了不少李白未道之细节，这也正如拍摄影视剧如《红楼梦》等，导演之手法也。此时，译者乃是导演，将李白之《静夜思》，愣生生搬上了银幕。

望月之 37：Longing for My Native Land in the Depth of Night（深夜，家的念想）

读英文

He was **in the depth of despair**.
他处于绝望的深渊。

The sea **is coated with** a film of raw sewage.
海上覆盖着薄薄一层未经处理的污水。

When we had tea, I could not **take my eyes from** her small delicate hands, the graceful way she moved, and her bright, black eyes expressionless in her clear face.
我们喝茶时，我不住地打量她，看她那纤纤小手、亮晶晶的黑眼珠、典雅的举止、清秀而没有表情的脸。

The police had **turned a blind eye to** the matter.
警方对那一事件视而不见。

A hummingbird is **poising** over the flower.
一只蜂鸟在花上盘旋。

No, nothing, not even **gossamer**-like traces.
我何曾留着像游丝样的痕迹呢？

The talk soon became impersonal, however, harking back to **the trails of**

childhood.

但他们的谈话很快就变得和个人无关了，大家开始追溯童年的记忆。

The crackle of an ember **accentuated the profound of silence that reigned**.

余烬中发出噼啪一声，突显出这一片沉沉的寂静。

英文散译

Longing for My Native Land in the Depth of Night

The depth of night sees me awake from my sound sleep: the floor seems to be frost-rimed when coated with crystal-encrusted frost. I take my eyes from the ground to turn an admiring gaze toward the moon wistfully: in the high sky a cold disked moon is poising, while beaming through the air which is a gossamer of glittering frost. Its silvery trail runs in a circle and never leaves the sky, and the forgotten trails of my childhood come back to me, when the silvery moon accentuates the profound of silence that reigns over this alien land and my native land.

英文诗译

Longing for My Native Land in the Depth of Night

The depth of night sees me
awake from my sound sleep:
the floor seems to be frost-
rimed when coated with
crystal-encrusted frost.
I take my eyes from the
ground to turn an admiring
gaze toward the moon
wistfully: in the high sky
a cold disked moon is
poising, while beaming
through the air which is
a gossamer of glittering
frost. Its silvery trail runs

in a circle and never leaves
the sky, and the forgotten
trails of my childhood come
back to me, when the silvery
moon accentuates the profound
of silence that reigns over this
alien land and my native land.

回译

深夜，家的念想
深夜，我醒来，
从酣睡之中：
地面——结霜，
似乎铺上一层
水晶外壳之霜。
我转移目光，
从地面，抬头望，
瞥见一轮月亮——
我欣赏，我怅惘。空中，
月儿，一如冷盘，
盘着旋，发着光；
飞度浩瀚长空，
恰似游丝闪，
又如流霜亮。
银迹白痕成圈圈，
旋于夜空朗。
童年旧事早遗忘，
而今又登场。
银月，无声白，
更显静谧与安详——
在他国，在故乡。

译人语

译诗对英文的借鉴，常有变通，并非照搬而拘泥不化。例如，The police had turned a blind eye to the matter（警方对那一事件视而不见），英译 to turn an admiring gaze toward the moon wistfully，不仅将宾语 eye 改成了 gaze，还把介词 to 改成了 toward。

A hummingbird is poising over the flower（一只蜂鸟在花上盘旋），令人想起词牌名"蝶恋花"的英译：butterfllies in love with flowers 或 butterfllies lingering over flowers。其实，可以采用动词 poise，改为：butterflies poising over flowers，这样就更加形象。因为 poise 作为动词，意为"保持……姿势；盘旋"。因有译诗：in the high sky a cold disked moon is poising（空中，月儿，一如冷盘，盘着旋）。

No, nothing, not even gossamer-like traces（我何曾留着像游丝样的痕迹呢？），其中的 gossamer，借用过来，便有译文：a gossamer of glittering frost（恰似游丝闪）。

最后的译文：the silvery moon accentuates the profound of silence that reigns over this alien land and my native land（银月，无声白，更显静谧与安详——在他国，在故乡）。写月亮照在诗人客居的屋内，也照在自己童年的故乡——正是一处月光，两处闲愁。

望月之 38：The Moon in a Deep Silent Night（静深之夜的月亮）

读英文

The **night deepened**.
夜色渐浓。

The rooms were lofty, **a ripple of sunshine flowed** over the ceilings.
房间很高，一道闪烁不定的阳光在天花板上移动。

A few rays **straggled in through** the opening of a deserted shaft.
几缕光线通过一个废井的井口散射进来。

The streets were deserted, save for a few random **stragglers**.
街上空荡荡的，只剩下稀稀拉拉的几个流浪者。

The sea was like oil, **the moon shone in all splendor**, and the Shark continued to sleep so soundly that not even a cannon shot would have awakened him.
海水就像油一样发亮，月亮发出盈盈光芒，而鲨鱼还在继续沉睡着，甚至连大炮都吵不醒它。

He was only **dimly** aware of it.
他只是模糊意识到这一点。

I can **dimly** recollect that in my earliest years I was the nursling of a goat, the death of which was a bitter grief to me.
我依稀记得在我很小的时候有只山羊喂养过我，它的死让我很悲伤。

英文散译

The Moon in a Deep Silent Night

The night deepens as the moon is wandering in the wide sky, whose light, as ripples of moonshine, is flowing stragglingly in through the holes of the thickly pasted window. A few rays, frosty on the ground, startle me from my fond dream, and I see a moon shining in all splendor. A gazer and a straggler, I begin to recall my dimly remembered distant homeland with lowered head ....

英文诗译

The Moon in a Deep Silent Night

The night deepens as
the moon is wandering
in the wide sky, whose
light, as ripples of moonshine, is flowing stragglingly
in through the holes of
the thickly pasted window.
A fcw rays, frosty on the
ground, startle me from
my fond dream, and I see
a moon shining in all splendor.
A gazer and a straggler,
I begin to recall my dimly
remembered distant home-
land with lowered head ....

回译

静深之夜的月亮
夜，沉沉深深，深深
沉沉；月儿，游荡在
广阔无垠的天空。月

之光，一道道，闪闪
烁烁，透过糊得厚厚
实实的窗户上的缝隙，
散射进来。几缕光线
照在地上，冰冷如霜，
把我从美梦之中惊醒
——只见月光盈溢。
我盯着，望着，惆着，
怅着，不觉忆起模糊
迷离、袅袅娜娜、缥
缈若梦的我的故乡——
于是我低头，垂眉……

译人语

对于译诗的理解，关键在于两个单词：stragglingly 及其同源词 straggler。这两个单词，均源于动词 straggle，含"分散；蔓延；散乱分布；掉队"之义。可用来描写光线，如上例句：A few rays straggled in through the opening of a deserted shaft（几缕光线通过一个废井的井口散射进来）；另外，还可用来描写具体的事物，例如：Vines are straggling over the fences（藤蔓在篱笆上爬着。）

动词之后，添加后缀-er，变成 straggler，大概意思是"流浪者；掉队者"。例如：The streets were deserted, save for a few random stragglers.（街上空荡荡的，只剩下稀稀拉拉的几个流浪者。）译诗采用 straggler，非汉语之"流浪者"或"掉队者"可对应，其中况味，竟没有一个汉语词语可尽情传达。另，译诗中，将 straggler 与 gazer 并置，作为 I 的同位语，致译文深有余味矣。

望月之 39：Still Night Yearning（静夜，思念）

读英文

Just then **a sort of brightness fell upon me** in the barrel, and looking up, I found the moon had risen and was **silvering** the mizzen-top **and shining white** on the luff of the fore-sail.

这时，一线光亮照进木桶，我看见月亮已经升起来了，在后桅纵帆的顶上洒下银色的光辉，把前桅帆也照得雪白。

A moon hung above the water like a silver plate.
一轮圆月就像银盘一样悬挂在水面上。

Everyone is **a moon**, and has dark side which he never shows to anybody.
每个人都是一个月亮，都有其不可展示给他人的阴暗面。

The doorway is shaped like **a moon**, a vase or a flower petal.
门洞有的像月亮有的像花瓶还有的像花瓣。

The bird stopped and hovered in **mid-air**.
这只鸟儿停下来，在半空中盘旋。

A lighthouse was flashing **afar** on the sea.
灯塔在远处的海面上闪着光。

英文散译

Still Night Yearning

Midnight finds me awake from a sound sleep when a sort of brightness is falling upon the strange ground before my strange bed, silvering it and shining white like frost and, looking up, I find a moon in the mid-air, which transports me afar, back to my home, my sweet home ….

英文诗译

Still Night Yearning
Midnight finds me awake
from a sound sleep when
a sort of brightness is
falling upon the strange
ground before my strange
bed, silvering it and
shining white like frost
and, looking up, I find
a moon in the mid-air,
which transports me
afar, back to my home,
my sweet home ….

回译

静夜，思念
半夜，从酣睡中
我醒来——
一线光亮，照
在陌生的地板上，
就在我陌生的
床前——将其
镀银，闪烁如霜。
抬眼望，只见
半空悬月，将
我的思绪拉远：

我梦回故乡，
我甜蜜的家乡……

译人语

英译若散文读之，一气流注：when，which 引起两个从句；and 之后使用逗号，也是典型的散文用法。另外，译文中，a sort of brightness（某种光亮），正译出"疑是地上霜"之状貌；随后的现在分词短语 silvering it and shining white like frost，描写生动。译文最后：my home, my sweet home....，叠词复语，强化故乡之思。

望月之 40：Still Night, Still Yearning（静夜，静思）

读英文

He awoke **chilled and sick**.

他醒了，感到又寒冷又难受。

In a little while, however, she again heard a little pattering of footsteps in the distance, and **she looked up eagerly**, half hoping that the Mouse had changed his mind, and was coming back to finish his story.

然而，过了一小会，她又听到远处传来轻微的脚步声，她眼巴巴地抬起头来，有点希望是老鼠改了主意，准备回来讲完故事。

…gazing at the last streak of color left by the setting sun; but there was no longer a sign of its glory to be **traced in the heavens** around her.

凝望着落日留下的最后一抹颜色，直到天空中再不见一丝霞光。

The medicine will **induce** sleep.

这种药会引起睡意。

They hoped their work would **induce** social changes.

他们希望自己的工作可以引起社会上的某些变化。

英文散译

Still Night, Still Yearning

I awake chilled and sick — chilled from the mid-night hoarfrost aground before my bed, and sick out of a dreamy homesickness which is pestering me. I look up eagerly, to trace the source of luminosity: the moon, solitary in the heavens, is a great inducer of nostalgia.

英文诗译

Still Night, Still Yearning
I awake chilled and
sick — chilled from
the mid-night hoarfrost
aground before my bed,
and sick out of a dreamy
homesickness which
is pestering me. I look
up eagerly, to trace the
source of luminosity:
the moon, solitary in
the heavens, is a great
inducer of nostalgia.

回译

静夜，静思
我醒来：寒冷，
不适——寒冷，
源自深夜床前
地板上的冷霜；
不适，源自挥之
不去梦幻似的
乡思。我，眼巴巴
地抬起头来，寻找
光明之源：噢，
月亮，孤孤独独

在空空的空中——
你是乡愁的引子！

译人语

　　"地上霜"，令人感到一丝寒冷；"思故乡"，令人心里难受。因此，英译可化用英文句子：He awoke chilled and sick（他醒了，感到又寒冷又难受。）英译采取复沓的形式：I awake chilled and sick — chilled from …, and sick out of ….，这样就有了强调的效果，诗意也得以凸出。"读英文"第三个句子中，to be traced in the heavens，在英译中被分开使用了：to trace the source of luminosity，以及 solitary in the heavens。动词 induce，在译文中变成了名词形式：inducer；而英文句子：the moon is a great inducer of nostalgia（月亮是乡愁的巨大诱导物），恰是耐人寻味之英文表达，汉译只表其大意，不能尽传其微妙之处。借鉴英文，创造性地借鉴英文，此译甚为明显。

望月之 41：Missing & Yearning in the Dead of Night（深夜之念想）

读英文

He awoke in his right mind, lying on his back on a rocky ledge.

他醒来时，头脑清醒，仰卧在一块岩石上。

Mine was a **heart** that **confined** itself to few objects, but dwelt upon those with the intenser passion.

我的爱好只局限在很少的事物上，但只要我喜欢上了，热情就会越来越强。

Slowly he followed it with his eyes, winding in wide sweeps among the bleak, bare hills, bleaker and barer and lower-lying than any hills he had yet encountered.

他的目光缓缓地跟随着河流望去。只见它蜿蜒流过一段宽广的河道，河两岸的小山荒芜光秃，比以往见过的任何小山还要荒芜、光秃、低矮。

The sun was **shining bright and warm**.

太阳发出明亮而温暖的光芒。

You may go or stay **according as** you decide.

你可要根据自己的决定而去或留。

Almost all Chinese who stay abroad for a relatively long time feel **great homesickness** for Chinese food.

几乎所有在国外生活很长时间的中国人，都会非常想念中国饭菜。

He closed his eyes for a while, then opened them. **Strange how the vision persisted!**

他闭了会眼睛，再睁开。奇怪的是，这种幻象竟依然存在！

His nerves had become blunted, numb, while **his mind was filled with weird visions and delicious dreams**.

他的神经已经变得迟钝、麻木，但他的脑海里却充满了不可思议的幻想和美好的梦境。

He **was aware of vague memories of** rain and wind and snow, but whether he had been beaten by the storm for two days or two weeks he did not know.

他依稀记得曾经有过冷雨、寒风和大雪，但是他到底被暴风雨吹打了两天还是两个星期，他已经记不得了。

He was surprised by **the triviality of** her anxieties.

她对琐碎小事的忧心忡忡使他感到惊讶。

英文散译

Missing & Yearning in the Dead of Night

Midnight sees me awake in my dreamy mind, which is confined in the strange room flooded with frosty moonlight. Slowly I trace the source of luminosity with my eyes, toward the high sky, to find a disc-shaped moon shining bright and cold; it stays motionless, seemingly to hear my heartbeat, on the quickening according as my homesickness is growing to be great, greater…. I close my eyes for a while, then open them. Strange how the visions persist! Lying back, my mind is filled with beautiful visions and delicious dreams of my native land, as I am aware of vague memories of the trivialities of my domestic life.

英文诗译

Missing & Yearning in the Dead of Night
Midnight sees me awake in
my dreamy mind, which is
confined in the strange room
flooded with frosty moonlight.

Slowly I trace the source of
luminosity with my eyes,
toward the high sky, to find a
disc-shaped moon shining bright
and cold; it stays motionless,
seemingly to hear my heartbeat,
on the quickening according
as my homesickness is growing
to bc great, greater…. I close my
eyes for a while, then open them.
Strange how the visions persist!
Lying back, my mind is filled
with beautiful visions and delicious
dreams of my native land, as I
am aware of vague memories of
the trivialities of my domestic life.

回译

深夜之念想
深夜见我醒来，思想
仍在梦中；围于陌生的
屋子里，沐浴在如霜的
月光中。慢慢，我慢慢
抬起惺忪之眼，寻找银
光之源——高高的空中，
只见一轮银盘：光亮，
冷淡。月亮一动不动，
似乎听见了我心跳的
节拍，越来越快，随着
我的乡愁渐增、渐浓……。
我闭上双眼，小憩一会，

然后睁开——幻觉幻象，

梦幻着月光，正是：玉户

帘中卷不去！再次躺平，

我魂归故乡，脑海里充盈着

美丽的幻想和美好的梦

境：袅娜依稀，家乡的

点点滴滴；仿佛恍惚，

故里的，滴滴，点点。

译人语

《静夜思》是五言绝句，才 20 个汉字，译文却 203 个字，正好十倍。似乎过分，但是，仔细想来，添加的，都是李白不曾道出的细节。正如将《静夜思》改编成电影，搬上银幕，译者便是导演。既然演出，细节便不可避免。例如，"围于陌生的屋子里"，才会"低头思故乡"；"慢慢，我慢慢抬起惺忪之眼，寻找银光之源——高高的空中，只见一轮银盘：光亮，冷淡。月亮一动不动，似乎听见了我心跳的节拍，越来越快，随着我的乡愁渐增、渐浓……"，正是"举头望明月"的特写镜头；接着，"我闭上双眼，小憩一会，然后睁开——幻觉幻象，梦幻着月光，正是：玉户帘中卷不去！"此乃特写镜头之延续；"再次躺平，我魂归故乡，脑海里充盈着美丽的幻想和美好的梦境：袅娜依稀，家乡的点点滴滴；仿佛恍惚，故里的，滴滴，点点。"通过蒙太奇手法，将"低头思故乡"的画面呈现出来。

回译散读，恰是一篇抒情散文。运用的，正是解构主义的翻译理念。有人担心解构翻译观会带来译者的随意性和任意性。但是，译文只要符合原诗之意，吻合原诗之情，就是合理的解读和翻译。解构主义翻译观的最大优点，是充分发挥译者的想象力和创造力，从而给出诗意充沛的译文来。

望月之 42：Languid Longing in the Depth of Night（深夜，思乡而憔悴）

读英文

He said, in his **languid** fashion.
他说道，一副没精打采的样子。

And **in the depth of** the sea we will dwell together.
我们一起生活在大海深处。

The moonlight bathed the scene in silver.
月光把一切镀成了银色。

The long morning and the longer afternoon **wore away** and the whistle blew for quitting time.
漫长的上午和更漫长的下午过去之后，下班的汽笛声响了起来。

The next morning **he was torn bodily** by his mother **from the grip of sleep**.
第二天早晨，约翰尼又被母亲从沉沉的睡梦中硬拖起来。

It always aroused him to frightened wakefulness, and for the moment, in the first sickening start, it seemed to him that he lay crosswise on the foot of the bed.
这事总是把他从睡梦中吓醒。在他刚刚被惊醒的、不舒服的那一刻，他似乎是横着睡在床脚。

A certain feeling of independence crept up in him, and the relationship between him and his mother changed.

他萌生了某种自食其力的感觉，接着他和母亲的关系开始发生了变化。

She tried her best **to poise herself**.

她尽全力使身体保持平衡。

The snow had ceased falling, and the air became **crisp and cold**.

雪已经停了，天气变得极其寒冷。

英文散译

Languid Longing in the Depth of Night

Through the window there is a glimpse of moonlight, which bathes the floor before my bed in silver, suggestive of hoarfrost aground. As the night wears away, a beam of moonlight, bright and brighter, by which I am torn bodily from the grip of sleep, arouses me to frightened wakefulness. And for the moment, in the first sickening start, it seems that a certain feeling of homesickness creeps up in me, as the moon is poising itself in the night sky 一 high, silent, crisp, and cold....

英文诗译

Languid Longing in the Depth of Night

Through the window there is
a glimpse of moonlight, which
bathes the floor before my bed
in silver, suggestive of hoarfrost
aground. As the night wears
away, a beam of moonlight,
bright and brighter, by which I
am torn bodily from the grip of
sleep, arouses me to frightened
wakefulness. And for the moment,
in the first sickening start,
it seems that a certain feeling
of homesickness creeps

up in me, as the moon is poising

itself in the night sky ——

high, silent, crisp, and cold….

回译

深夜，思乡而憔悴

透过窗户，一瞥

月光，把我床前

的地板，镀成银色，

令人想起大地

之霜。夜，深深

沉沉，一束月光，

越来越亮，把我

从沉沉的睡梦中

硬拖起来，从睡

梦中惊醒。一刹

那间，一种不适

的感觉；然后，

思乡的感觉萌生。

夜空中，一轮明月

正演练着平衡——

高，静，清，冷……

译人语

英译中，which bathes the floor before my bed in silver；the night wears away；I am torn bodily from the grip of sleep；arouses me to frightened wakefulness；in the first sickening start；a certain feeling of homesickness creeps up in me；the moon is poising itself in the night sky —— high, silent, crisp, and cold….等，都是语言亮点。回译也只是基本达意而已，显然不如英文巧妙。读英文而巧借鉴，才有望把汉诗英译提高到英诗的高度。

望月之 43：Midnight Moon: Throes of Homesickness（思乡之苦，在深夜）

读英文

He had two years longer to serve, but two years were too long for him **in the throes of homesickness**.

他还要工作两年，但是这两年对饱受思乡之苦的他来说太长了。

It was a cry that began, muffled, **in the deeps of sleep**, that swiftly rushed upward.

这一叫喊声刚开始时是沉睡中的低声嘟囔，接着很快提高了声调。

"You'll be late," she said, under the impression that **he was still stupid with sleep**.

"你要迟到了。"母亲说道，她以为他还睡得稀里糊涂的。

His earlier memories lingered with him, but he had no late memories.
那些过去的记忆常常萦绕在他的脑海里，可是近来的事他却记不得了。

Strive as he would to hide it, a growing anxiety was manifest, but Li Wan, **groping after the words with which to paint the picture**, took no heed.

虽然他努力地想要掩饰，但脸上还是渐渐地露出了些许焦虑，可是李婉正在脑海里苦苦找寻词语来形容自己的梦境，并没注意到他的表情。

She eyed it wistfully, grasping its virtues at a glance and thrilling again at the unaccountable sensations it aroused.

她渴望地看着那木屋，一下就明白了它的好处，那些无法言喻的感受又令她激动起来。

英文散译

Midnight Moon: Throes of Homesickness

A beam of dazzling light, frostlike, steals into my room, which awakes me from the deeps of my sleep, with which I am still stupid. The memories from my fond dream still linger with me, when I, groping after the words with which to paint the picture, glance and gaze at the midnight moon wistfully, in the throes of homesickness.

英文诗译

Midnight Moon: Throes of Homesickness

A beam of dazzling light,
frostlike, steals into my room,
which awakes me from
the deeps of my sleep,
with which I am still
stupid. The memories from
my fond dream still linger
with me, when I, groping after
the words with which to paint
the picture, glance and gaze at
the midnight moon wistfully,
in the throes of homesickness.

回译

思乡之苦，在深夜
一束炫目的月光，
如霜，潜入屋内，
把我从沉睡中惊醒，
脑子依然稀里糊涂。

美梦的记忆，
还在脑海里萦绕，
我苦苦找寻词语，
来形容刚刚逝去
的梦境；同时，
抬眼望见月亮，
我渴望，我凝望——
思乡之苦，在深夜。

译人语

英译中，which awakes me from the deeps of my sleep；the memories from my fond dream still linger with me；groping after the words with which to paint the picture 等，因有英文之借鉴，而成为靓句。动词"望"字，英译 glance and gaze，一词而双译，且押头韵：一盯一看，一短暂一延长，恰好。结尾用介词短语 in the throes of homesickness，与诗题呼应。

望月之 44：Midnight: Helpless Nostalgia（午夜：无助的乡愁）

读英文

There was one other **memory of the past, dim and faded**, but **stamped into his soul everlasting** by the savage feet of his father.

关于过去的记忆里还有一件事，虽然有些模糊不清了，但他父亲那双野蛮的脚还是永远铭刻在了他的灵魂深处。

"Where?" she finally asked, removing the apron from her head and **gazing up at him with a stricken face in which there was little curiosity.**

她拉下脸上的围裙，愁苦却几乎毫不惊奇地抬头盯着他，最后她问道："你要去哪里？"

His muscles relaxed and **he sank back**, an exultant satisfaction in his eyes which he turned from her so that she might not see.

他的肌肉放松了下来，向后躺去，眼中闪现出一种欣喜和满意的神情，他背过身，好不让李婉看见。

They both sat silent and looked at poor Alice, who felt ready **to sink into the earth**.

然后他们两个静静地坐在那里，看着可怜的艾丽丝，看得她直想钻到地下去。

The prince had not the least knowledge of the way to Waq of the Caucasus, and

was cast down by the sense of his helplessness.

王子完全不知道去高加索的沃格的路，他因无助而陷入沮丧。

英文散译

Midnight: Helpless Nostalgia

Glitteringly, glaringly, dazzlingly, strikingly, the moonbeam penetrates my window, through frosty air, onto the ground before my bed, and into my fond dream, where there are so many memories of the past, dim and faded, but everlastingly stamped into my soul. Awake, I gaze up at the moon with a stricken face in which there is much sentimentality and, as I sink back in my bed, I sink into helpless nostalgia.

英文诗译

Midnight: Helpless Nostalgia

Glitteringly, glaringly, dazzlingly,
strikingly, the moonbeam penetrates
my window, through frosty air, onto
the ground before my bed, and into
my fond dream, where there are
so many memories of the past,
dim and faded, but everlastingly
stamped into my soul. Awake, I gaze
up at the moon with a stricken face
in which there is much sentimentality
and, as I sink back in my bed,
I sink into helpless nostalgia.

回译

午夜：无助的乡愁
闪闪，烁烁，炫炫，耀耀，
月光——破窗而入，刺穿
霜冷的空气，落在床前的

地板之上，进入我的美梦
之乡。梦中，多少昔日的
记忆，虽然模糊不清，却
永远铭刻在我灵魂的深处。
一觉醒来，我抬头看着
月亮，满脸的愁苦，
满脸的伤感。当我
回躺床上，无助的乡愁，
如同潮水，将我淹没……

译人语

英译第三和第四行中，through，onto，into，三个介词的使用，非常巧妙；回译中，变成了动词："刺穿"、"落在"、"进入"。前两个动作实写，第三个动作则是虚写：into my fond dream（进入我的美梦之乡），诗意顿生。译诗的最后两个单词 helpless nostalgia，借鉴自最后一个英文句子：The prince had not the least knowledge of the way to Waq of the Caucasus, and was cast down by the sense of his helplessness.（王子完全不知道去高加索的沃格的路，他因无助而陷入沮丧。）显然，这里变化较大：由 the sense of his helplessness（无助的感觉），联想到 helpless nostalgia（无助的乡愁）这样的搭配：巧妙，非汉语所能尽言。

此诗回译发朋友圈，林克难教授评曰："我欣赏这种先诠释再翻译的做法。中国古诗里的意境，外国读者是无法从直译过去的字里行间读得出来的。智中替他们做了诠释的工作，用文字描绘出诗的意境，很有必要，趟出了一条译诗新路，值得中国译界关注。这是古诗英译的崭新路径，为中国文学走出去开拓了一条新路。"

望月之 45：Frosty Night: A Fond Dream of My Native Land（霜冷之夜：梦回故里）

读英文

The sun **shines brightly**.
阳光灿烂。

Dewdrops **shine brightly** in the sunshine.
露珠在阳光下闪闪发光。

He took **an upward glance at** the helicopter.
他举目向直升机一瞥。

He strained his eyes to **catch a glimpse of** the president.
他竭尽目力想看总统一眼。

As he spoke, the tree across the street **appeared** with dazzling brightness **on his inner vision**.
他一面说着，一面觉得街对面的那棵树在他的心里似乎放出了耀眼的光。

But **her thoughts were far away**, across the Ice Mountains **to the east, to the little corner of the earth where her childhood had been lived**.
但是她的思绪飘得很远，穿过冰山去了东方，去了那个她儿时生活过的角落。

英文散译

Frosty Night: A Fond Dream of My Native Land

The moon, frostlike, is shining brightly and gently into my room, when gently I awake from a fond dream. Upward glancing, I catch a glimpse of a bright moon: it must be also shining on my native land, which is now appearing on my inner vision. My thoughts are far away, over rills after rills and across hills upon hills, to the little corner of the earth where my childhood has been lived.

英文诗译

Frosty Night: A Fond Dream of My Native Land

The moon, frostlike, is shining
brightly and gently into my room,
when gently I awake from a fond
dream. Upward glancing, I catch a
glimpse of a bright moon: it must
be also shining on my native land,
which is now appearing on my
inner vision. My thoughts are
far away, over rills after rills
and across hills upon hills, to
the little corner of the earth where
my childhood has been lived.

回译

霜冷之夜：梦回故里
月亮，如霜，灿兮烂兮，
温柔照入我的房间——
我轻轻，轻轻从美梦中
醒来。抬眼望，只见一轮
明月：此刻，她，一定也
照在我故乡的土地之上

——故乡，此刻正浮现
在我的心头之上。我思绪
飘扬，飞过千山，跨越
万水，来到地球上那个
小小的地方——在那儿，
我度过了美好的童年时光。

译人语

英译中，三个句号，三个句子；《静夜思》则是四个句子。翻译，当然是一种重写，尤其中国古典诗歌的英译；不重写，则无法译出成功的译作。再看句法，插入成分，如 frostlike；分词短语，如 upward glancing；介词短语，如 over rills after rills 和 across hills upon hills；从句运用，如 when，which，where 等引导的从句，这些都使译文接近地道之英文。

汉语古典诗歌，多一行是一行，常单而独之；英文诗歌，则诗行缠绵交错，难以完整摘录。观中国古诗之英译者，常行行对应；如此语言异化，译诗则难以在英语世界产生良好的阅读效果。语言归化，是译诗打动读者的基本条件。

望月之 46：Midnight Fancies
（午夜的幻想）

读英文

Thus **amusing himself with fancies**, he came to the field.

就这样，他一边快乐地幻想着，一边走向了那块土地。

What do you want **at this hour of night**?

这深更半夜的，你想干什么？

As Tom waxed old, however, **he grew thoughtful**.

可是，汤姆逐渐老了，心事也逐渐重了。

And **we solaced ourselves** during the warm sunny hours of mid-day under the shade of a broad chestnut, on the cool grassy carpet that swept down to the water's edge.

在这炎热的中午，我们在一棵大栗树底下的阴凉处，坐在一直延伸到河边的绿毯子上，享受起来。

While **I was musing upon these matters** my companions had spread a repast, from the contents of our well-stored pannier.

当我想着这些事的时候，我的伙伴们从装的满满的食篮里拿出了食物铺开。

英文散译

Midnight Fancies

The floor before my bed seems to be frosty with a beam of moonlight, which is stealing through the window. In flight of thoughts stirred by the bright wheel of moon in the high sky, I am amusing myself with fancies at this hour of night, when I grow thoughtful, solacing myself by musing upon family matters of my remote native place of long ago.

英文诗译

Midnight Fancies

The floor before my bed

seems to be frosty with

a beam of moonlight, which

is stealing through the window.

In flight of thoughts stirred

by the bright wheel of moon

in the high sky, I am amusing

myself with fancies at this hour

of night, when I grow thoughtful,

solacing myself by musing upon

family matters of my remote

native place of long ago.

回译

午夜的幻想

床前的地板上，

似乎，被月光涂上了

一层冷霜——月光

正从窗户悄悄潜入。

一轮明月，悬于清冷

的高空，引发阵阵

乡愁：我幻着，想着，

乐呵着，在这深更，

在这半夜——心事

渐重，遥想久远的

故乡，昔日家庭生活的
点点滴滴，聊以自慰。

译人语

译诗题目：《午夜的幻想》，是的，静夜思，正是一首午夜幻想曲。回不去的青春，回不去的故乡。于是，"遥想久远的故乡，昔日家庭生活的点点滴滴，聊以自慰。"这，难道不是《静夜思》的别样解读吗？从英文散译来看，译诗由两个句子构成，第二个相对复杂，正写望月者的复杂情思。仔细看来，亦不乏内韵，如译诗开头：floor，frosty，before（重音在第二个音节），押头韵；同时，before 又与 bed，be 等，形成头韵。另外，amusing myself with fancies（乐呵着）和 solacing myself by musing upon family matters（聊以自慰），稍有重复，起到了强调的作用。

望月之 47：Midnight Moon & Lust for Home（午夜之月·家的渴望）

读英文

Davy moaned, lifting his head and watching them dance **in the slanting rays of the su**n.

戴维抬起头，看着他们在斜阳的光辉下跳舞。

And **a dim light crept through** the windows of the pagoda.

昏暗的光束小心翼翼地穿出寺庙的窗户。

And the unknown, muttering to himself, **directed his steps towards** the kitchen.

陌生人一边自言自语，一边朝厨房走去。

A strange calm wrapped about them.

一种异常的平静包围着他们。

But his wound had **rendered** him too weak to support such an exertion.

但是他身上还有伤，而且很虚弱，根本禁不起这样的折腾。

And now **they were feeling the rough edge of the country**.

现在他们感受着在这个乡村生活的艰辛。

Grubless, spiritless, **with a lust for home in their hearts**, they had been staked by the P. C. Company to cut wood for its steamers, with the promise at the end of a passage home.

他们饥肠辘辘，无精打采，非常想回家。他们受到 P.C.公司的资助，为它的汽船伐木，公司承诺最后会给他们回家的路费。

英文散译

Midnight Moon & Lust for Home

The floor before my bed is bathed in the slanting rays of the moon which, frostlike, are creeping through the window. When I direct my eyes towards the moon, a strange calm begins to wrap about me, rendering me forgetful of the rough edge of a wandering life, with a lust for home arising in my heart ....

英文诗译

Midnight Moon & Lust for Home

The floor before my bed

is bathed in the slanting

rays of the moon which,

frostlike, are creeping

through the window. When

I direct my eyes towards

the moon, a strange calm

begins to wrap about me,

rendering me forgetful of

the rough edge of a wandering

life, with a lust for home

arising in my heart ....

回译

午夜之月·家的渴望
床前的地板，
沐浴在月照的
斜光之中——
如霜，小心翼翼，
穿窗而入。举目

望月，一种异常
的宁静，开始将
我包围，让我
忘记游子生活的
艰辛，心生念想：
我的家，哦，我
内心深处的家……

译人语

《静夜思》，实乃游子想家之作。多年漂泊流浪在外，"游子生活的艰辛"，见月而得以消解；并有"一种异常的宁静，开始将我包围"。正是午夜之月，最能引发游子对于家的渴望。英文而言，is bathed in，are creeping through the window，direct my eyes towards the moon，a strange calm begins to wrap about me，forgetful of the rough edge of a wandering life，a lust for home arising in my heart 等，都是鲜活地道之英文措词与表达。

望月之 48：Reverie in the Night of a Dead Silence（幻想：死寂的夜晚）

读英文

There was **a dead silence** instantly.

外面立即陷入死一般的沉寂。

I know **I was roused** at six o'clock **by** the call to my supper, and I looked about dazed, to discover **the long rays of the late afternoon sun streaming across the valleys**.

六点钟的时候，有人唤我吃晚饭，我被叫醒了，一脸的茫然，发现傍晚斜长的日光正撒遍山谷。

She boldly drew near to Λramis's **shutter**, and tapped at three equal intervals with her bent finger.

她毅然走到阿拉米的百叶窗前，朝窗子用相同的节奏地敲了三下。

I was trying to **shut out** the noise.

我试着把噪音关在外面。

The field **was covered with rime** in the early morning.

清晨地里覆盖着一层白霜。

Her imagination carried her far off, and showed her innumerable dangers.

她的想象将她带到了远处，让她看到无数危险。

Imber's **head drooped** once more, and his eyes went dull, as though a film rose up and covered them from the world.

英勃尔的头又垂下去，他的双眼变得模糊，好像生了一层薄膜，看不见周围的世界。

She sat there **with her head drooping**.

她垂着头坐在那儿。

And the unknown **fell into a reverie** which lasted some minutes.

陌生人沉思了几分钟。

Then, **as her thoughts strayed back to the scene of the sacrifice**, and recalled the dangers which still menaced her, she shuddered with terror.

接着，当她回想祭祀的情景，回想那些至今还对她的生命存在威胁的危险时，她就害怕得颤抖起来。

I dare say even I've done one or two rash things **in my dim and distant youth**.

我敢说年轻时我也干过一两件轻率的事儿。

It appears we are out of the mini-crisis with the Liverpool fiasco **an increasingly dim and distant memory**.

似乎我们已经走出了那段小危机，完败给利物浦的那场比赛变成愈发遥远而淡泊的回忆。

英文散译

Reverie in the Night of a Dead Silence

I am roused in the depth of night by the long rays of the cold moon streaming through the shutter, which fails to shut out the light. I look about dazed, to discover the ground silvered with a cover of rime. I lift my head toward the bright moon, when my imagination carries me far off and, head drooping, I fall into a reverie as my thoughts stray back to the scene of my home, the home in my dim and distant youth.

英文诗译

Reverie in the Night of a Dead Silence

I am roused in the depth of night

by the long rays of the cold moon

streaming through the shutter,

which fails to shut out the light.
I look about dazed, to discover
the ground silvered with a cover
of rime. I lift my head toward
the bright moon, when my imagination
carries me far off and, head drooping,
I fall into a reverie as my thoughts
stray back to the scene of my home,
the home in my dim and distant youth.

回译

幻想：死寂的夜晚

深夜，斜长的冷月之光，
穿过百叶窗，撒落进来，
把我惊醒；百叶窗未能
把光线挡在屋外。茫茫
然，我环顾四周，发现
地面好像镀上了一层银
色的白霜。举目望月，
我心飞翔，浮想联翩
——然后，垂头，沉思：
我的思想，回到了家乡
的现场——遥远而迷离
的，我的童年的，家乡。

译人语

"斜长的冷月之光……把我惊醒"，当然是诗意的搭配：月光把人惊醒，可见月光之魅。比较英译和回译，汉语显然不如英文。例如，英译中 shutter 一词，源于动词 shut，又与 shut out 形成同源；discover 与 cover，也有同源关系，终至译文颇堪回味。另外，my imagination carries me far off，I fall into a reverie，my thoughts stray back to the scene of my home 等，都是很好的英文表达方式。

最后，dim and distant，很早就用过这样的组合，大胆的尝试而已；现在读到英文里完全类同的用法，倍感惊喜。

望月之 49：Rimed Longing in Meditative Silence of the Night（深夜默想，思念如霜）

读英文

Age has rimed his once black hair.
岁月给他当年的黑发蒙上了一层白霜。

He smoked in **meditative silence**.
他抽着烟，默默地沉思。

I wake in the night with a startle.
夜里我突然惊醒。

He **startled from sleep**.
他从睡梦中惊醒起来。

And **a dim light crept through the windows** of the pagoda.
昏暗的光束小心翼翼地穿出寺庙的窗户。

Fix, seated in the bow, **gave himself up to meditation**.
菲克斯坐在船头沉思着。

He felt a sort of insurmountable longing to abandon the game altogether.
他觉得心中有一种无法克制的渴望，那就是彻底退出这场游戏。

英文散译

Rimed Longing in Meditative Silence of the Night

I wake in the night with a startle from my sleep, to find a silvery light creeping through the window, to rime the floor before my bed, when my once black hair has already been rimed by age. Sitting up and gazing at the bright moon, I give myself up to meditation, while feeling a sort of insurmountable longing, a longing for my native land, for my native home ….

英文诗译

Rimed Longing in Meditative Silence of the Night

I wake in the night with a
startle from my sleep, to find
a silvery light creeping through
the window, to rime the floor
before my bed, when my once
black hair has already been
rimed by age. Sitting up and
gazing at the bright moon, I give
myself up to meditation, while
feeling a sort of insurmountable
longing, a longing for my native
land, for my native home ….

回译

深夜默想，思念如霜
夜里，我突然从梦中
惊醒，只见一束银色
之光，小心翼翼，穿
窗而入，给我床前的
地板，蒙上了一层白
霜。而我曾经的青丝，

也被岁月染而成霜。
坐起，凝视月亮，我
尽情沉思，内心升起
一种无法抑制的渴望：
渴望着，我的故土；
渴望着，我的故乡……

译人语

李白的地上之霜，在译诗中得以放大：不仅"我床前的地板，蒙上了一层白霜"，而且"思念如霜"，而且"我曾经的青丝，也被岁月染而成霜"。"少小离家老大回，乡音未改鬓毛衰"——而这里，译诗所表达的，却是鬓毛已衰，却依然客居他乡，只能低头沉思："内心升起一种无法抑制的渴望：渴望着，我的故土；渴望着，我的故乡……"。

英文诗题中，Rimed Longing（如霜的思念）和 Meditative Silence（沉思默想）极具诗意。诗中再次两用动词 rime，带来较好的美学效果。最后的两个 longing，具顶针效果；for my native 的复用，加强了语气；变异的 land 与 home，其实是 homeland 之拆解：新意滋生。

望月之 50：Silvery Moon & Fantasy （银月·幻想）

读英文

A heavy, copper-colored beam of light came in at the west window, gilding the outlines of the children's heads **with** red gold.

一道浓重的橘黄色光线透过西窗射了进来，给孩子们的头上勾勒出一圈火红金黄的轮廓。

He lowered his eyes before that calm and frank look.

看到福格先生平静而坦诚的目光，他还是低下了头。

While each of the party **was absorbed in reflections** so different, the sledge flew fast over the vast carpet of snow.

当每个人都专注地想着截然不同的心事时，雪橇正快速地飞越广袤无垠的雪地。

At first **his countenance was illuminated with pleasure**, but as he continued, thoughtfulness and sadness succeeded; at length, laying aside the instrument, **he sat absorbed in reflection**.

起初，他脸上洋溢着笑容，但弹着弹着，表情便变得深邃、忧伤。最后，他把吉他搁置一旁，坐在那里沉思着。

His eyes were **somber**, resentful and yet nervous.

他的眼睛显得阴沉、愤懑，然而又惶惶不安。

He **fantasies** himself a doctor.

他想像自己是一位医生。

He could now leave Fort Kearney station, and **pursue his journey homeward in peace**.

他可以现在就离开卡尼堡车站，平平安安地回家。

英文散译

Silvery Moon & Fantasy

A cold, silvery beam of light comes in at the window, gilding the floor before my bed with hoarfrost. I lift my eyes towards the bright moon, and sit up absorbed in reflection, my countenance somber with homesickness, fantasying myself a pursuer of my journey homeward ....

英文诗译

Silvery Moon & Fantasy

A cold, silvery beam

of light comes in at

the window, gilding

the floor before my

bed with hoarfrost.

I lift my eyes towards

the bright moon, and sit

up absorbed in reflection,

my countenance somber

with homesickness, fantasy-

ing myself a pursuer of

my journey homeward ....

回译

银月·幻想

一道冷银色

的光线，透过

窗户射了进来，
给我床前的
地板，镀上一层
白霜。举目，凝
望月亮；起坐，
沉思冥想。面容
沉郁，因为思乡：
想象着，自己是
赶路人，走在，
回家的路上……

译人语

诗题《银月·幻想》，虽无原题之"静夜"，但"银月"和"幻想"却是译诗内容的关键词；在译诗中独成体系，上下联通。如此诗题，当然合理合情。标题之外，此译简洁而佳，英文尤胜。借鉴之时，常有变通。例如，第二个英文句子：He lowered his eyes before that calm and frank look，译文中，反其意而用之，改成 I lift my eyes towards；将随后的第三到第七个英文句子综合运用，译写出这样一个句子来：and sit up absorbed in reflection, my countenance somber with homesickness, fantasying myself a pursuer of my journey homeward ....；特别是，把动词 pursue，改写成名词 pursuer，正符合英文喜欢用-er 后缀类单词的特点：比英文更英文。

望月之 51：The Midnight Moon: Meditative Eyes & Meditative Mood（午夜之月：沉思的目光，内心的冥想）

读英文

She stood looking at him with **meditative** eyes.
她站着用沉思的目光打量他。

She found him in a **meditative** mood.
她见他正在沉思。

A sunbeam **stole through** the crack between the window and the black-out curtains and **shone straight on to** my bed.
一束阳光穿过窗户与遮光窗帘之间的缝隙，直接照到我的床上。

The instant that I had crossed the threshold the door slammed **heavily** behind us.
我一跨进门槛，门就在我身后砰的一声重重关上。

The years have silvered her hair.
岁月已使她的青丝似雪。

英文散译

The Midnight Moon: Meditative Eyes & Meditative Mood
A moonbeam steals through the window and shines straight on to my bed,

silvering the room and riming the floor, when the years, spent far away from my dear home, have heavily silvered my hair. Upward looking at a bright moon with meditative eyes, I find myself in a meditative mood.

英文诗译

The Midnight Moon: Meditative Eyes & Meditative Mood

A moonbeam steals
through the window
and shines straight on
to my bed, silvering
the room and riming
the floor, when the years,
spent far away from my
dear home, have heavily
silvered my hair. Upward
looking at a bright moon
with meditative eyes, I find
myself in a meditative mood.

回译

午夜之月：沉思的目光，内心的冥想
一束月光，轻轻
悄悄，穿过窗户，
直照在我的床上，
给屋子镀银，
给地面上霜。
离别家乡的岁月啊，
使我青丝如雪，
青丝，如雪！
抬望眼，只见
一轮明月——

沉思的目光，噢，

内心的冥想……

译人语

译诗诗题《午夜之月：沉思的目光，内心的冥想》，似乎正是《静夜思》之解构。英译中，silvering the room 与 riming the floor，平行结构；回译中，"给屋子镀银，给地面上霜"，节奏铿锵。"离别家乡的岁月啊"，借鉴自贺知章《回乡偶书》第二首中的诗句："离别家乡岁月多"。副词 heavily，似乎不太好译，便采用了反复的技巧："使我青丝如雪，青丝，如雪！"效果颇佳。随后的 meditative eyes 和 meditative mood，原译"沉思的目光"和"冥想的情绪"，后来改为"沉思的目光"和"内心的冥想"，不仅押韵，搭配也更合理；同时，还呼应了诗题。

望月之 52：Silent Night & Domestic Tranquility（宁静的夜晚，恬静的家庭生活）

读英文

The western end **was** already **bright with moon beams**.
西方上面已为月光照得明亮了。

He gave "Harry, old boy," to understand that these three girls were **a source of** the greatest anxiety and worry to him. Enough to drive a man distracted.
他告诉"哈里老弟"，那三个女儿是他最大的心事和烦恼。简直快把人逼疯了。

…gazing at the last streak of color left by the setting sun; but there was no longer a sign of its glory to be **traced in the heavens** around her.
凝望着落日留下的最后一抹颜色，直到天空中再不见一丝霞光。

She was punctual to the rendezvous, and shouts of welcome greeted her on all sides, as her pale beams **shone gracefully in the clear heavens**.
月亮准时赴约，四面八方的欢呼声直上青天。晴朗的天空中，月亮幽幽地散发出皎洁的光芒。

The only object that I could distinguish was the bright moon, and **I fixed my eyes on** that with pleasure.

我唯一能辨认的物体就是那皎洁的月亮，我满心欢喜地凝视着它。

There was no bitterness in him, nothing but **an inordinate hunger for rest**.
他的心中没有伤悲，只是极度渴望休息。

My value for **domestic tranquility** should much exceed theirs.
我应该远比他们重视家庭的平静生活。

英文散译

Silent Night & Domestic Tranquility

The floor before my bed is bright with frostlike beams, of which the source is traced to the bright moon, which is shining gracefully in the clear heavens. When I fix my eyes, through the lattice window, on the moon which poises itself in the silent night sky, there is nothing in me but an inordinate hunger for domestic life of tranquility.

英文诗译

Silent Night & Domestic Tranquility

The floor before my bed is
bright with frostlike beams,
of which the source is
traced to the bright moon,
which is shining gracefully
in the clear heavens. When I
fix my eyes, through the lattice
window, on the moon which
poises itself in the silent night
sky, there is nothing in me
but an inordinate hunger for
domestic life of tranquility.

回译

宁静的夜晚，恬静的家庭生活
床前的地上，

有光线，明亮
如霜。追光求源
——皎皎空中，孤月
一轮，正幽幽散发着
皎洁的光芒。当我——
透过花格之窗，
凝视着悬于宁静的
夜空之中的月亮，
我心无旁骛，只是
渴望——渴望着，
恬静的家庭生活。

译人语

译文 The floor before my bed is bright with frostlike beams，借鉴自英文 The western end was already bright with moon beams（西方上面已为月光照得明亮了）；如果采用 moon beams，正吻合原文"床前明月光"，但是，既然明言"月光"，怎么还"疑是地上霜"呢？显然，原诗前后逻辑上有点矛盾。不过，李白也只能这样。如果不用"明月光"，该怎么说呢？似乎没有更好的方法。译诗中，去掉 moon，改用 frostlike beams（如霜的光线），就可以避免这样的矛盾，效果显然好多了。

另外，在对英文句子的借鉴中，译文多有变通。例如，of which the source is traced to the bright moon, which is shining gracefully in the clear heavens，借鉴了两个英文句子中的词语，并灵活运用。再如，When I fix my eyes, through the lattice window, on the moon which poises itself in the silent night sky，在短语 fix my eyes on 的中间，加上插入成分，译文语言更具英文形断意连之味道。最后，将英文短语 domestic tranquility 改成 domestic life of tranquility，更符合《静夜思》之意境。

望月之 53：Frosty Moon Filled with a Longing for Home（霜月：盈溢着家乡的思念）

读英文

Frosty windows make great surfaces for children to draw on.
有霜的窗户是孩子们画画的好地方。

His face beamed like a full moon.
他的脸像一轮圆月般散发着光芒。

She **eyed it wistfully, grasping its virtues at a glance and thrilling again at the unaccountable sensations it aroused.**
她渴望地看着那木屋，一下就明白了它的好处，那些无法言喻的感受又令她激动起来。

She **beamed at** me.
她对我微笑。

The **tired brain** is **tranquilized** in sleep.
疲惫的脑在睡眠中得到宁静。

Because of the growth of **brain and mind**, people know more and more about the infinitesimal of themselves and the infinity of surrounding.
因为随着大脑的发育，心灵的成长，人类会越来越认识到自身的无限小，环境的无限大。

英文散译

Frosty Moon Filled with a Longing for Home

The moon is beaming through the frosty window, onto my bedside floor which is now rimy, as my face is beaming like a full moon, filled with a longing for home. I eye the moon wistfully, grasping its virtues at a glance and thrilling at the unaccountable sensations it arouses. We beam at each other, the moon and me, and my childhood moon in particular, is the tranquilizer of my tired brain and exhausted mind.

英文诗译

Frosty Moon Filled with a Longing for Home

The moon is beaming through the
frosty window, onto my bedside
floor which is now rimy, as my face
is beaming like a full moon, filled
with a longing for home. I eye the
moon wistfully, grasping its virtues
at a glance and thrilling at the
unaccountable sensations it arouses.
We beam at each other, the moon
and me, and my childhood moon
in particular, is the tranquilizer of
my tired brain and exhausted mind.

回译

霜月：盈溢着家乡的思念
月亮闪烁着，穿过如霜
的窗户，照在我床前的
地上，覆盖如霜。我的脸
也发光，像那圆圆的月亮——
盈溢着家乡的思念。我

渴望地看着月亮，一下就
明白了它的好处，那些无法
言喻的感受，令我激动起来。
我们相互微笑着：月亮和我。
月亮，我童年的月亮，
是我疲惫的大脑和精疲
力竭的内心的——镇静剂。

译人语

译文中，I eye the moon wistfully, grasping its virtues at a glance and thrilling at the unaccountable sensations it arouses，借鉴自英文：She eyed it wistfully, grasping its virtues at a glance and thrilling again at the unaccountable sensations it aroused（她渴望地看着那木屋，一下就明白了它的好处，那些无法言喻的感受又令她激动起来），几乎是"拿来主义"：只是改变了主语的人称，动词的时态，并去掉副词 again。在读英文的过程中，有时碰到一个句子，就眼睛一亮，尤其是联想到一句古诗的时候。另外，We beam at each other, the moon and me（我们相互微笑着：月亮和我），如此英译，因为联想到李白的诗句："相看两不厌，只有敬亭山"（《独坐敬亭山》）。最后，my childhood moon in particular, is the tranquilizer of my tired brain and exhausted mind，译文中的 tranquilizer，当为亮点，借鉴自英文句子：The tired brain is tranquilized in sleep（疲惫的脑在睡眠中得到宁静）。英文善用 -er 后缀类词汇，如此借鉴，正显译者之创造性。

望月之 54：The Moon & My Hometown & Me（月亮·故乡·我）

读英文

The three blows were scarcely struck when the inside casement was opened, and **a light appeared through the panes of the shutter**.

刚敲过三下，里面的那层窗子就打开了，灯光从百叶窗的缝隙里透了出来。

The mist **penetrated into** the room.

雾气渗进了室内。

Further, this woman, as if not certain of the house she was seeking, **lifted up her eyes to look around her**, stopped, went a little back, and then returned again.

而且，那个女人似乎不知道自己要找的到底是哪个屋子。她不断抬头环视四周，走走停停，折回去，又倒回来。

In a little while every sound ceased but his own voice; **every eye fixed itself upon him**; with parted lips and bated breath the audience hung upon his words, taking no note of time, rapt in the ghastly fascinations of the tale.

不一会儿，除了他在讲话，所有声音都停止下来，每只眼睛都注视着他。人们张着嘴，屏住呼吸，兴致盎然地听他讲着，全然忘记了时间，沉浸在这个恐怖却引人入胜的故事中。

The old man's eyes **beamed with an expression of gentle affection**.

老人的眼睛带着温柔的表情眨了眨。

Sister St. Joseph's broad simple **face**, with its red cheeks, was **beaming**.
圣约瑟修女那张淳朴的大脸红红的面颊上都是笑意。

英文散译

The Moon & My Hometown & Me

A midnight light appears on the panes of the shutter, penetrates into the room, and falls onto the floor of my bedroom, which is silvered like frost. I lift up my eyes to look around me, until they fix themselves upon a bright moon, which is beaming at me with an expression of gentle affection, and my face is now beaming back. The distance between us, between the moon and me, is narrowing, narrowing down, as my native land is drawing near to me, and I am approaching my hometown ....

英文诗译

The Moon & My Hometown & Me

A midnight light appears on the
panes of the shutter, penetrates
into the room, and falls onto
the floor of my bedroom,
which is silvered like frost.
I lift up my eyes to look around
me, until they fix themselves
upon a bright moon, which is
beaming at me with an expression
of gentle affection, and my face
is now beaming back. The distance
between us, between the moon
and me, is narrowing, narrowing
down, as my native land is
drawing near to me, and I am
approaching my hometown ....

回译

月亮·故乡·我

午夜之光，从百
叶窗的缝隙里透
过，进入屋里，
落在卧室的地上：
如银，似霜。举
目四望——聚焦
在一轮明月之上。
月亮正看我，柔
情似水，而我的
脸，也笑意相迎。
月亮和我，我们
之间的距离，在
缩小，渐缩渐小
——我的故乡，正
靠近我，我也正在
靠近我的故乡……

译人语

英译中，I lift up my eyes to look around me, until they fix themselves upon a bright moon，这里的 they 和 themselves，都指"眼睛"（eyes）：眼睛把自己固定在明月之上——如此举目四望而聚焦，何其鲜活的表达！随后，which is beaming at me with an expression of gentle affection, and my face is now beaming back（月亮正看我，柔情似水，而我的脸，也笑意相迎），又联想到李白诗句"相看两不厌，只有敬亭山"（《独坐敬亭山》）。这也呼应了译文的最后：as my native land is drawing near to me, and I am approaching my hometown ....（我的故乡，正靠近我，我也正在靠近我的故乡……）。我思故乡，故乡思我；我爱故乡，故乡爱我。这也该是李白《静夜思》秘而不宣的吧。

望月之 55：A Splash of Light & a Touch of Homesickness（一束亮光 · 乡思之病）

读英文

Moon gazing is an ancient art.
观月是一门古老的艺术。

When his gaze slid down my body in a slow, smooth way, I silently blessed the designer of the red dress for sharing their talents with the world.
当他的目光，缓慢而顺滑地，从我的身体上下滑之时，我心里默默祝福这红色衣服的设计者，他们跟这世界分享了他们的艺术才华。

Suzie bent down **to meet my gaze**.
苏西弯下身，迎合我的目光。

She **softened slightly**.
她感到稍微有点感动。

I **slightly melted** under her stare.
在她的注目之下，我感到有点融化了。

英文散译

A Splash of Light & a Touch of Homesickness
A splash of light on my bedside floor — moonlight? or hoarfrost? When my

gaze slides up in a slow, smooth, steady way, to meet the moon's gaze, I silently start to long for my home, my dear home which is now dim and distant, and I am softened and melted, slightly first, then heavily, by a touch of homesickness.

英文诗译

A Splash of Light & a Touch of Homesickness

A splash of light on my
bedside floor — moon-
light? or hoarfrost? When
my gaze slides up in a slow,
smooth, steady way, to meet
the moon's gaze, I silently
start to long for my home,
my dear home which is
now dim and distant, and
I am softened and melted,
slightly first, then heavily,
by a touch of homesickness.

回译

一束亮光 · 乡思之病
一束亮光洒在床前
的地上——月光？
冷霜？我的目光，
缓慢而平稳地上滑，
去迎合明月之光，
我便开始思乡，
悄悄地，思念我亲爱
的故乡：袅袅娜娜，
隐隐约约，逶迤遥远。
我感动，我融化：

情渐深，意渐浓——
噢，这，这乡思病！

译人语

译诗标题"A Splash of Light & a Touch of Homesickness"中，前半部分 a splash of light，来自译诗的开头；后半部分 a touch of homesickness，来自译诗的结尾。暗含因果关系：因了这"一束亮光"，点亮了"这乡思病"。抛开汉语诗题，在英译中再造，需要译者竭力用心，方可望产生良好效果。

英译中，大量运用元音韵和头韵等。例如，light, my, bedside, moonlight, slides 押元音韵；splash, slides, slow, smooth, steady 押头韵；way 与 gaze 押元音韵；meet 与 moon 押头韵；silently 与 start 押头韵；dear, dim, distant 押头韵；softened 与 slightly 押头韵；同时，softened, and, melted 押单词尾韵；而 slightly 又与 heavily 押单词尾韵。再加上 my home 与 my dear home 的反复，译诗的音韵效果非常明显。

望月之 56：Homebound Thoughts, from a Strange Floor（返乡的思绪，自陌生的卧室地面）

读英文

His gaze felt warm as it started on my face and **trailed down to** the jersey and then my legs.

他看着我的脸，然后，温暖的目光移到我的毛线衫上，再移到我的腿上。

See how they **awaken responsiveness in children**.

瞧他们如何唤醒孩子们的反应。

Jaxson glanced at me quickly before **he dropped his gaze again** and shrugged.

贾克森很快看了我一眼，然后垂下目光，耸了耸肩。

His gaze dropped to me, and the intensity in his green eyes did crazy things to the butterflies in my stomach.

他目光下落，看着我，绿色的眼瞳聚精会神地看着我，让我坍塌不安。

He is a **homebound** traveler.

他是个返乡的旅客。

英文散译

Homebound Thoughts, from a Strange Floor

My gaze feels warm as it starts on the floor before me, which is frosty from a bright beam of moonlight, and trails up, through the lattice window, to the bright moon in the boundless blue night sky, as it awakens nostalgia in me, when my gaze drops back to the strange floor, my homebound thoughts flying and drifting away ….

英文诗译

Homebound Thoughts, from a Strange Floor

My gaze feels warm as
it starts on the floor before
me, which is frosty from
a bright beam of moonlight,
and trails up, through
the lattice window, to the
bright moon in the bound-
less blue night sky, as it
awakens nostalgia in me,
when my gaze drops back
to the strange floor, my homebound
thoughts flying and drifting away….

回译

返乡的思绪，自陌生的卧室地面
我的目光温暖——
当我睁眼看到床前的
地面：一束月光流照
而下，如霜；然后，
目光穿过花格之窗，
寻到一轮明月，悬于
无边无际蓝色的夜空
——月亮唤醒我内心
的乡愁，我的目光也
回落到这陌生卧室的

地面之上，返乡的

思绪，飞啊，飞扬……

译人语

第一个英文句子很好：His gaze felt warm as it started on my face and trailed down to the jersey and then my legs. （他看着我的脸，然后，温暖的目光移到我的毛线衫上，再移到我的腿上。）《静夜思》的动作：先看卧室里如霜的地面，然后抬头望月——动作缓慢。借用英文时，将 trail down to 与前面的表述分开使用，插入一个定语从句；把 trail down 反其意而用之，改成 trail up 之后，也没有马上使用介词 to，再次插入介词短语 through the lattice window，然后才出来 to，这样就使英文表达更具英文之味道。正是：散文之语言，诗歌之内容。

另外，将英文句子 See how they awaken responsiveness in children （瞧他们如何唤醒孩子们的反应），改译成 it awakens nostalgia in me，也需要译者一定的诗歌联想和语言变通能力。

望月之 57：Midnight Moonlight: Cold Frost, or Warm Light?（午夜的月光：冷霜？暖光？）

读英文

Suzie clung to the edge of the pool, **her gaze fixed on** Jaxson.
苏西依靠在池塘边缘，目光盯着贾克森。

I leaned my back against the door and **tipped my face upward**.
我背靠着门，仰脸向上。

I heard Jaxson's soft chuckle as he nodded and then **slipped his gaze over to** me.
我听见贾克森轻轻的笑声——他点头，然后目光向我看过来。

Ashley **kept her gaze on** the floor, obviously uncomfortable with our disagreeing in front of her.
艾什莉目光盯着地面，面对我们的分歧，她显然感觉不太舒服。

Suddenly, **my mind opened up a memory, one I'd tucked away years ago** for my own survival.
突然，我的思想开启了一个回忆，多年前，为了自己的生存，我把这事藏在心底。

A memory flashed in my mind. One that was **soft and sweet, innocent really.**

I was wrapped in a warm light.

我的脑子里闪过一个回忆：温柔，甜蜜，单纯。温柔之光，将我包围。

英文散译

Midnight Moonlight: Cold Frost, or Warm Light?

Light — moonlight? or cold frost? In a trance my gaze fixes on the floor for a moment before I tip my face upward, to slip my gaze over to the moon, on which my gaze is kept. Suddenly, my mind opens up a memory, one I have tucked away dozens of years ago, soft and sweet, innocent really, when I am still a child of my native land, and I am wrapped in a warm light ....

英文诗译

Midnight Moonlight: Cold Frost, or Warm Light?

Light — moonlight? or cold
frost? In a trance my gaze fixes
on the floor for a moment before
I tip my face upward, to slip
my gaze over to the moon, on
which my gaze is kept. Suddenly,
my mind opens up a memory,
one I have tucked away dozens
of years ago, soft and sweet,
innocent really, when I am still
a child of my native land, and
I am wrapped in a warm light ....

回译

午夜的月光：冷霜？暖光？
光——月光？冷霜？
恍惚之中，我的目光
聚焦地面之上；
片刻之后，我仰头

向上，目光看向月亮，
久久凝望。突然，我
的思想开启了一个回忆，
几十年前，我把它在
心底珍藏：温柔，甜蜜，
单纯——那时，我还是
故乡的孩子啊，温柔
之光，将我包围……

译人语

译诗标题:《午夜的月光：冷霜？暖光？》，颇耐寻味，令人想起曾经流行的《走天涯》中的歌词："谁的眼泪在月光中凝聚成了霜？是你让我想你想断肠"。歌曲虽是情歌，但故乡也正是我们终生不渝的情人啊。

"冷霜"，乃"疑是地上霜"之"霜"；"暖光"，乃"床前明月光"之"光"。"离别家乡岁月多，近来人事半销磨。"贺知章如是慨叹。在外打拼，客居他乡，游子的冷暖，唯有自知。那陌生的土地上，一定有冷霜；月是故乡明——那午夜的月亮，总令人想起故乡，从而心生暖意，因此，月光，总是暖光。

"我在仰望，月亮之上，有多少梦想在自由地飞翔？昨天遗忘啊，风干了忧伤，我要和你重逢在那苍茫的路上。生命已被牵引，潮落潮涨，有你的远方，就是天堂。"凤凰传奇唱的《月亮之上》，情深意切，感人肺腑。为什么我们对月亮如此向往？因为她代表着我们内心的美好与单纯，那是我们失落已久的天堂。

望月之 58：A Straggler in a Moonlit Night（月光琅照独夜人）

读英文

He ran his hands through his hair as **he kept his gaze focused on the floor**.
他眼睛盯着地面，手指穿过头发。

When **my gaze made its way over to** the little square on the floor, an idea formulated itself in my mind.
当我的眼睛看见地上的小方块之时，我脑子里产生了一个念头。

Will any one **without the walls of Paris** understand it?
巴黎以外的人是否能懂得这部作品呢？

She raised her eyebrows as **her gaze locked with mine**.
她与我四目相对，一脸的惊奇。

He paused and studied me. But he didn't look relieved. Instead, **his gaze hardened**.
他停下来，仔细看我。但他一点也没放松，相反，他的目光凛厉起来。

"I think I'm a little lost," I said, taking note of **the lingering gaze** the nanny shot my direction.
"我想我有点迷茫了，"我说着，注意到保姆看向我的流连的目光。

I stilled, **the memory of** that sweet kiss on graduation night and this one **blending together to forever brand me** as hers.

我僵住了，毕业晚上甜蜜亲吻的回忆，叠加着这次亲吻，注定我是她的人了。

The short winter day was nearly ended. The streets were deserted, save for a few random **stragglers**.

冬季的天很短，马上就要黑了。街上空荡荡的，只剩下稀稀拉拉的几个流浪者。

But it grows dark: the crowd has gradually dispersed, and only a few **stragglers** are left behind.

但是，天黑了。人群渐渐散去，只留下几个掉了队的人。

英文散译

A Straggler in a Moonlit Night

I keep my gaze focused on the bedside floor, which is rimy, frosty, or silvery with light? From the moon? When my gaze makes its way over to the bright moon without the window, I find her gaze locked with mine, both softened, affectionately lingering. The memory of maternal cares and the tenderness of moonlight blend together to forever brand me as a son of my hometown, though a straggler now.

英文诗译

A Straggler in a Moonlit Night

I keep my gaze focused
on the bedside floor,
which is rimy, frosty,
or silvery with light?
From the moon? When
my gaze makes its way
over to the bright moon
without the window, I find
her gaze locked with mine,
both softened, affectionately
lingering. The memory of

maternal cares and the tenderness of moonlight blend
together to forever brand me
as a son of my hometown,
though a straggler now.

回译

月光琅照独夜人
我眼睛盯着床前的
地面：如霜，似银，
因光——源自月亮？
当我移动目光，
看见窗外的明月，
我发现：月光
与我的目光，光光
相对，软化下来，
情深，流连，徘徊，
惆怅。母爱的记忆，
掺和着柔和的月光
——我的身心早被
烙印：我是家乡的
儿子啊，虽然在这
月光琅照的晚上，
我是个独夜之人。

译人语

英文句子：He paused and studied me. But he didn't look relieved. Instead, his gaze hardened.（他停下来，仔细看我。但他一点也没放松，相反，他的目光凛厉起来。）其中，his gaze 与动词 harden 的搭配，极好。不过，《静夜思》中，我看月亮，月亮看我，其光必然柔和。因此，借鉴之时，反其意而用之：harden 变成了 soften；同时，把两个句子中的两个单词 soften 和 lingering 结合在一起使用，并添加副词 affectionately，译文成为: I find her gaze locked with mine, both softened, affectionately lingering，这就接近一个地道而向佳的英文句子了。

另一个英文句子也很好: I stilled, the memory of that sweet kiss on graduation night and this one blending together to forever brand me as hers.（我僵住了，毕业晚上甜蜜亲吻的回忆，叠加着这次亲吻，注定我是她的人了。）英译适当改写，变成: The memory of maternal cares and the tenderness of moonlight blend together to forever brand me as a son of my hometown, though a straggler now，似乎来自英语作家笔下。最后两个英文句子中的 straggler，可印证此句中 straggler 的用法。回译时，把 straggler 译为"独夜之人"，也是权宜之计；其实，此一英文单词的内在含义，不可用汉语词语对等译出，也难以尽列详述。想起杜甫《旅夜书怀》中的名句："飘飘何所似，天地一沙鸥。"一叹！

望月之 59：Still Night & Immortal Light（静夜·永恒之光）

读英文

The boyfriend's moony face peered out between **the blinds**.
那个男朋友呆呆的脸，透过百叶帘往外看。

It is an emanation from **the distant orb of immortal light**.
它是从远处那个发出不灭之光的天体上放射出来的。

Then he glanced back at me, **his gaze roaming over my body**.
然后他向我看过来，目光在我身上游弋。

Jaxson chuckled **as his gaze roamed over me**.
贾克森咯咯地笑了，他的目光在我脸上扫来扫去。

She raised her eyebrows as **her gaze locked with mine**.
她与我四目相对，一脸的惊奇。

I had to have faith that **there were parts of our past that lingered in the back of her mind**.
我不得不相信：她的脑海里，有着我们过往的一些记忆。

英文散译

Still Night & Immortal Light
The floor before my bed is silvery with light, suggestive of hoarfrost; I glance

up through the blinds to trace the source, and I see a distant orb of immortal light, whose gaze is roaming over me, to be locked with mine. Awakened are parts of my past youthful days that linger in the back of my mind.

英文诗译

Still Night & Immortal Light
The floor before my bed
is silvery with light,
suggestive of hoarfrost;
I glance up through the
blinds to trace the source,
and I see a distant orb of
immortal light, whose gaze
is roaming over me,
to be locked with mine.
Awakened are parts of my
past youthful days that linger
in the back of my mind.

回译

静夜·永恒之光
我床前的地上，光亮
如银，令人想起大地
之霜。透过百叶窗，
我往外看，试图寻找
光之源——只见遥远的
夜空中，有个发着永恒
之光的天体，其光在我
身上游弋，与我的目光，
光光相对。就这样，唤醒
我对于过往的一些回忆：

那青春年少的岁月，鲜
活着——在我的脑海里。

译人语

"窗户"的英文，借用第一个英文句子里的 blinds（百叶窗），可联想到古代比较考究的窗户。用 a distant orb of immortal light（遥远的发着永恒之光的天体）来指代月亮，不仅仅是为了陌生化效果，也可联想到"我"与月亮的陌生感：久违而永恒的月亮。

英文句子 She raised her eyebrows as her gaze locked with mine.（她与我四目相对，一脸的惊奇。）在上个译文中就使用过了，这里再用，因其表达太好。此译中，另外一处比较好的借鉴，是英文句子 I had to have faith that there were parts of our past that lingered in the back of her mind.（我不得不相信：她的脑海里，有着我们过往的一些记忆。）译文改为：Awakened are parts of my past youthful days that linger in the back of my mind.（唤醒我对于过往的一些回忆：那青春年少的岁月，鲜活着——在我的脑海里。）于是，译文语言增彩不少。

望月之 60：Midnight: Gazing & Moon-Gazing（午夜之望：望月）

读英文

My gaze fell on Jaxson, who stood near the exit.
我的目光落在贾克森身上，他站在出口处。

Jaxson parted his lips as **his gaze swept from Liam to Mason**.
随着目光从利亚姆游弋到梅森身上，贾克森张大了嘴巴。

Her face was contorted in a look of pity as **she swept her gaze over** my messy hair and rumpled pajamas.
当她的目光扫过我乱蓬蓬的头发和皱褶的睡衣，她的脸都走样了：一副可怜兮兮的样子。

There was a hint of mystery in his eyes, and **his gaze swept over me**.
他眼里透出一丝神秘之气，目光从我身上扫过。

His eyes swept the room.
他把室内扫视了一遍。

He swallowed and I saw **a flash of fear in his gaze**.
他抑制住情感，我看见他眼里闪过一丝恐惧。

"I have great news," I said, hoping **to lift the worry off her**.
"有好消息，"我说，希望打消她的担心。

英文散译

Midnight: Gazing & Moon-Gazing

My gaze falls on the frosty floor before my bed, from which my gaze gradually sweeps to the moon, where I see a flash of care and concern in her gaze, with a vain hope to lift the nostalgia off me.

英文诗译

Midnight: Gazing & Moon-Gazing

My gaze falls on the frosty
floor before my bed, from
which my gaze gradually
sweeps to the moon,
where I see a flash of
care and concern in her
gaze, with a vain hope to
lift the nostalgia off me.

回译

午夜之望：望月
我的目光落在床前如霜
的地上，然后，慢慢
游弋到月亮之上——
月亮正盯着我看，
我感到了关切与关爱
的月光，以及月亮的
痴心和妄想：希望我
不再受苦，不再思乡。

译人语

英文句子中，好几个都与描写目光相关，例如：My gaze fell on Jaxson, who stood near the exit.（我的目光落在贾克森身上，他站在出口处。）Jaxson parted his lips as his gaze swept from Liam to Mason.（随着目光从利亚姆游弋到梅森身

上，贾克森张大了嘴巴。）Her face was contorted in a look of pity as she swept her gaze over my messy hair and rumpled pajamas.（当她的目光扫过我乱蓬蓬的头发和皱褶的睡衣，她的脸都走样了：一副可怜兮兮的样子。）There was a hint of mystery in his eyes, and his gaze swept over me.（他眼里透出一丝神秘之气，目光从我身上扫过。）His eyes swept the room.（他把室内扫视了一遍。）He swallowed and I saw a flash of fear in his gaze.（他抑制住情感，我看见他眼里闪过一丝恐惧。）

这六个句子中，都含有 gaze（最后一个 eyes），搭配的动词，多是 sweep，个别用 fall on。而与 sweep 搭配时，可用 gaze 作主语，也可用 gaze 作宾语，比较灵活。"读英文"中，给出了较多的英文例子，有些不一定用在译文中，读者自可体会。总之，译文中多次描写到"看"，但英文却不用一个 look，因其抽象笼统。采用 gaze 与 sweep 等词，便形象生动多了。

望月之 61：Mind Stilled in the Still Night（思想宁静：在宁静之夜）

读英文

Still the Mind: An Introduction to Meditation
《静思：冥想导论》

She **peers through the mist**, trying to find the right path.
她透过雾眯着眼看，想找出正确的路。

She **peers at me** over the top of her glasses.
她从眼镜上方盯着我看。

My entire body heated as **I forced my gaze upwards**.
我强迫自己往上看，整个身体都感到发热。

He **rested a curious gaze on** the strange woman.
他好奇地盯着那个怪异的女人看。

The boy **looks with wistful eyes at** the toy on display.
那男孩看著展出的玩具，眼中流露出渴望的神情。

The poor mother **has wistful reminiscences of** her lost youth.
这个贫穷的母亲怅惘地回忆她已经逝去的青春。

Such wishful thinking of theirs will never be realized.
他们的这种痴心妄想是永远也不会实现的。

Let's not waste a precious second on **wishful thinking** or useless regrets. Life really is too short.

我们不要将宝贵的时间浪费在痴心妄想或作无谓的惋惜上，生命实在是
太短暂了。

The countryside is very **tranquil**, with less people.
乡下挺安静的，人没那么多。

The story took place in a **serene** summer night.
故事发生在一个宁静的夏夜。

He registered **irrepressible** joy.
他流露出压抑不住的喜悦。

You've got into **wild flights of fancy**.
你的想象力太丰富了。

英文散译

Mind Stilled in the Still Night

My bedside floor is white with hoarfrost, whose source of light is traced to the moon peering at me through the lattice window, as I slowly lift my eyes upwards, to rest a gaze, wishful and wistful, on the tranquil moon, in such a serene, silent, still night — and my mind is stilled, except for irrepressible homebound wild flights of fancy.

英文诗译

Mind Stilled in the Still Night
My bedside floor is white
with hoarfrost, whose source
of light is traced to the moon
peering at me through the
lattice window, as I slowly
lift my eyes upwards, to rest
a gaze, wishful and wistful,
on the tranquil moon, in such
a serene, silent, still night —
and my mind is stilled, except

for irrepressible homebound

wild flights of fancy.

回译

思想宁静：在宁静之夜
床前的地上，因霜
而白亮，追其光源——
原来是月亮，她在
悄悄看我，穿过这花格
之窗。慢慢地，我抬头
望月，目光充满着渴望
与怅惘，看着恬静的
月亮，在这宁宁静静、
平平淡淡的晚上，
我的思想也宁静下来
——除了压抑不住的
对于家乡的狂想。

译人语

译诗标题 *Mind Stilled in the Still Night*，第一个 still 用作动作，第二个 still 用作形容词，从而带来诗的回味，也强调了深夜之"静"。英文句子 My entire body heated as I forced my gaze upwards（我强迫自己往上看，整个身体都感到发热）中，只是借用了副词 upwards，有了译文：I slowly lift my eyes upwards。随后的译文，to rest a gaze, wishful and wistful, on the tranquil moon, in such a serene, silent, still night，头韵效果明显：wishful 与 wistful，such，serene，silent，still 等，构成两组头韵。另外，译诗第一行中的 bedside 与 white，第二行中的 hoarfrost 与 source，第五行中的 window 与 slowly，都押元音韵；第七行中的 wishful 和 wistful，既头韵又尾韵，最后一行中的 flights 与 fancy，也押头韵。

整首译诗，用一个英文句子表达，主句更兼从句、短语，插入另有头韵、元音韵，一气流注，酣畅淋漓，仿佛李氏太白之直抒胸臆。

望月之 62：Midnight: a Sudden Urge of Nostalgia（**深夜：乡思深涌**）

读英文

He leaned closer all the while, **keeping his gaze on me**.

同时，他靠得更近了，目光盯着我。

Imber listened **for a space**, when **a wonderment rose up in his face** and he broke in abruptly.

英勃尔听了一会儿，脸上露出诧异的神情，便突然插嘴道。

The Indians looked at him **in wonderment** that he should laugh.

印第安人惊奇地看着他，不知道他为何大笑。

The nanny scoffed **as she dropped her gaze** and made her way over to the dresser to fiddle with the items there.

保姆嘲笑着，垂下了目光，走向碗柜，开始摆弄里面的物件。

I lifted my chin, **reveling in the sudden urge of** confidence **that shot through my veins**.

我扬起下巴，陶醉于自己一时的自信，这心血来潮的自信。

英文散译

Midnight: a Sudden Urge of Nostalgia

I keep my gaze on the bedside floor, frosty and rimy, for a space, a wonderment rising up in my face which, lifted upward, is filled with moonbeams. Then I drop my gaze, lost in the sudden urge of nostalgia that shoots through my veins.

英文诗译

Midnight: a Sudden Urge of Nostalgia

I keep my gaze on

the bedside floor,

frosty and rimy,

for a space, a wonder-

ment rising up in my

face which, lifted up-

ward, is filled with

moonbeams. Then I

drop my gaze, lost in

the sudden urge of

nostalgia that shoots

through my veins.

回译

深夜：乡思深涌

我目光盯着

床前的地上：

如霜；顷刻

之间，脸上

露出诧异的

神情。我仰头

遥望——满脸

的月光。然后，

垂下目光，迷失于

一时的乡愁——

这乡愁啊，

令我热血沸腾。

译人语

　　英文标题 *Midnight: a Sudden Urge of Nostalgia* 中，a sudden urge of 的表达很好；相应的回译中，《深夜：乡思深涌》，重复的"深"字，才有点诗意。汉英语言，各有优势。最后一句英文很好：I lifted my chin, reveling in the sudden urge of confidence that shot through my veins.（我扬起下巴，陶醉于自己一时的自信，这心血来潮的自信。）英译借鉴后，适当改写：Then I drop my gaze, lost in the sudden urge of nostalgia that shoots through my veins。把 reveling（陶醉），改成 lost（迷失）；把 the sudden urge of confidence（一时的自信）改成 the sudden urge of nostalgia（一时的乡愁），恰到好处。

　　译诗由两个句子组成，一长一短：第一个长句大体对应《静夜思》之前三行，第二个短句大体对应最后一行"低头思故乡"。《静夜思》之英译，关键不在译文字，贵在译情，贵在译出《静夜思》之深情。正是：乡思深深深何处？深夜见月情自浓。

望月之 63：Late Night & Total Homesickness（夜深深，思乡浓）

读英文

She is **keeping her gaze downturned**.

她目光一直看着地上。

Immediately the thumping began again — very loud at first but soon fainter and fainter, till it died out **in the direction of** the sea.

重击声马上又开始了——起初很响，不过很快就虚弱下来，慢慢地，朝着大海的方向，消失了。

He nodded and lifted his hand **in Suzie's direction**.

他点点头，举起手，朝着苏西的方向。

She **held Katie's gaze**.

她吸引着卡蒂的目光。

The distant mountain **holds my gaze**.

远山吸引着我的目光。

Their business misfortune **had reduced the family to a state of total despair**.

他们生意上的噩运，让全家陷入了彻底的绝望之中。

英文散译

Late Night & Total Homesickness

I keep my gaze down-turned, at the bedside white floor — hoarfrost? Or moonlight? Slowly I lift my eyes in the direction of the moon, which holds my gaze for quite a moment. And I am reduced to a state of total homesickness, homebound thoughts flying and soaring ….

英文诗译

Late Night & Total Homesickness

I keep my gaze down-
turned, at the bedside white
floor — hoarfrost? Or
moonlight? Slowly I lift
my eyes in the direction
of the moon, which
holds my gaze for quite
a moment. And I am
reduced to a state of
total homesickness,
homebound thoughts
flying and soaring ….

回译

夜深深，思乡浓
我目光一直盯着
地上，看着床前
白色的地面——
冷霜？还是月光？
慢慢地，我举目
望去，朝着月亮
的方向；月亮吸引着
我的目光，时间久长。
然后，我陷入浓
浓的乡思之中：

向往家乡的情思，

飞呀，飞扬……

译人语

译诗标题 *Late Night & Total Homesickness*，在英文中，尚可；若回译成《深夜与彻底的思乡》，则言语乖舛；现译《夜深深，思乡浓》，正符合汉语言语之习惯。译诗三句，发问开端：hoarfrost? Or moonlight?（冷霜？还是月光？）恰吻合"疑是地上霜"之疑问口气。没有直言"床前明月光"，以避免李白开头两个诗句之逻辑矛盾。

译诗最后一句：And I am reduced to a state of total homesickness, homebound thoughts flying and soaring ….，句号之后使用 and，英文里其实常见，比较文气，但中国译者不太常用，因为英文读得少的缘故。A state of total homesickness，表述地道；homebound thoughts flying and soaring，连用两个动词的现在分词形式，强调者也，与汉语回译之"飞呀，飞扬"，旗鼓正相当，铢两恰悉称。

望月之 64：Deep into the Night, Deep into Homesickness（深夜情浓，急欲回家乡）

读英文

They danced **deep into the night**.
他们跳舞直至深夜。

I experienced **deep homesickness**.
我经历了浓浓的乡思。

"My, you have grown up," she said as **she ran her gaze over me** like an adoring parent.

"噢，你长大了啊，"她一边说着，一边眼睛上下打量着我，像个慈爱的母亲。

After Lottie informed me that my mother was staying at the McKnight mansion and that we were breaking up, I really didn't **have a desire to head home** anytime soon.

洛蒂告诉我，母亲一直呆在麦克奈特公寓，家里面临分崩离析，之后我就没有一点儿想要赶快回家的欲望了。

She **is heading home** today.
今天她就回家。

英文散译

Deep into the Night, Deep into Homesickness

I run my gaze over the bed-side strange floor which is frostily rimy with a silver beam of light, the source of which is traced upward, through the lattice window, toward a bright moon in the boundlessly blue sky, the familiar moon of my childhood, and I have a sudden desire to head home ….

英文诗译

Deep into the Night, Deep into Homesickness

I run my gaze over the bedside strange floor which
is frostily rimy with a
silver beam of light, the
source of which is traced
upward, through the lattice
window, toward a bright
moon in the boundlessly
blue sky, the familiar
moon of my childhood,
and I have a sudden
desire to head home ….

回译

深夜情浓，急欲回家乡
我走眼溜光，
盯着床前——
陌生的地上：
一束银色之光，
将其照得朦胧
似霜。求其源，
抬头望，穿过

花格窗：一轮
明月高空悬，
恰似年少家乡！
故乡之月皎皎兮，
急欲回家乡。

译人语

英文句子 They danced deep into the night（他们跳舞直至深夜）中，deep 是副词；I experienced deep homesickness（我经历了浓浓的乡思）中，deep 是形容词。无论词性，用法很好。借鉴后，便有了译文标题：*Deep into the Night, Deep into Homesickness*，明显有了平行结构（parallelism）的修辞效果，自然佳译。汉语回译：《深夜情浓，急欲回家乡》，单看平淡无奇，其实，重在与译诗最后一行的"急欲回家乡"产生勾连。

回译首行"我走眼溜光"，措词新颖，与英文 run my gaze 正相匹配，动感顿生。英译不易；回译，有时也靠灵感。综观回译，韵律铿锵："光"、"上"、"光"、"霜"、"望"、"窗"、"乡"、"乡"——音节响亮；读之，则有宋词风味。

望月之 65：Dark Night & Moon of My Native Land（深夜偶见故乡之月）

读英文

The nanny **glanced down at** my hand **and then back up to meet my gaze**.
保姆目光下垂，看着我的手，然后抬头看着我的眼睛。

The dog **is white with** brown **splashes**.
狗一身白毛，夹有棕色的斑块。

She moved to London **in search of** fame and fortune.
她为了追逐名利，搬迁到了伦敦。

Our **native land** is as pretty as a picture.
祖国河山美丽如画。

Exiles long to return to their **native land.**
流亡者们渴望回到自己的祖国。

英文散译

Dark Night & Moon of My Native Land

I glance down at the bed-side floor, which is white with frost-like silvery splashes of light, and then straight up to meet the gaze of the moon through the window. The dark night has given me a pair of dark eyes, with which I am in search of the moon, the bright moon of my native land.

英文诗译

Dark Night & Moon of My Native Land

I glance down at the bed

-side floor, which is white

with frost-like silvery

splashes of light, and

then straight up to meet

the gaze of the moon

through the window.

The dark night has given

me a pair of dark eyes,

with which I am in search

of the moon, the bright

moon of my native land.

回译

深夜偶见故乡之月

我目光下垂，

看着床前的

地面：银白似霜，

因了亮光之烁烁

闪闪；然后，

我举目——透过

窗户——迎看

月光。黑夜给了

我一双黑色的

眼睛，我却用它

寻找月亮——

我故乡的月亮。

译人语

译诗标题 *Dark Night & Moon of My Native Land*，将黑夜与故乡之月并列，

形成对比。客居在外，常见黑夜，而能够照亮黑夜的，却是故乡之月。同时，标题中的黑夜，与诗歌随后出现的"黑夜给了我一双黑色的眼睛"做个铺垫，形成前后呼应。当然，这个句子借鉴自顾城的名句："黑夜给了我黑色的眼睛，我却用它寻找光明。"此句不乏悲情，而故乡之思，同样也是人生之注定，何尝不是带有悲情的成分呢？英文标题如此，回译却是：《深夜偶见故乡之月》，文字显然没有对应，但对应的，却是内在的诗思与诗情。

韵律而言，同样有韵，例如 which is white with 之头韵，the moon through the window 之元音韵，-side，white，-like，light，night，eyes，bright 等之元音韵。汉诗英译，若只知尾韵，则为门外之汉矣。

望月之 66：Homesickness in a Dead Silence（死寂中的乡愁）

读英文

The room **falls into an uncomfortable silence**.
房间静了下来，令人感到不安。

Her eyes dart down for a second.
她的眼睛往下看了一会。

I look at it instinctively, my lips curving up.
我本能地看着它，撅着嘴唇。

Her eyes drift away for a second.
她的目光一时移开了。

My gaze lands in Dad.
我的目光落在爸爸身上。

The air between us is as cold as her glare.
我们之间的空气，也像她的目光一样冰冷。

Her brows crease in confusion.
她的眉头皱了起来。

He let out a sigh.
他叹了一口气。

Her joyful expression switching into a thoughtful one.
她的表情从快乐变成了沉思。

I can't let my depression **come back to haunt me**.
我不能让沮丧之情再次缠绕着我。

英文散译

Homesickness in a Dead Silence

My room falls into a dead silence, in the dead of night, as the moonlight falls, through the window, into my room, onto the floor which seems to be frostily coated with a thin film. My eyes dart up instinctively to be drifting away, and my gaze lands in the moon, as the gaze of the moon lands in me — the air between us is as cold as her glare. My brows crease in confusion, and I let out a sigh when my frame of mind is switched into a thoughtful one — homesickness comes back to haunt me.

英文诗译

Homesickness in a Dead Silence

My room falls into a dead
silence, in the dead of night,
as the moonlight falls, through
the window, into my room,
onto the floor which seems to
be frostily coated with a thin film.
My eyes dart up instinctively
to be drifting away, and my gaze
lands in the moon, as the gaze
of the moon lands in me —
the air between us is as cold as
her glare. My brows crease in
confusion, and I let out a sigh
when my frame of mind is switched
into a thoughtful one — homesickness comes back to haunt me.

回译

死寂中的乡愁
深更夜半之时，我的

房间陷入死寂——
月光，透过窗户，
落入我的房间，
照在屋里的地上，
似乎着上一层薄薄
的白霜。我本能地
抬眼望，目光移开，
落在月亮之上，而月亮
之光，也照在我的身上。
我和月亮，我们之间
的空气，也冰冰冷冷，
恰似月光。我的眉头
皱起，一声叹息，当我
的思绪进入沉思——
思乡之情再次缠绕着我。

译人语

译诗采取了特写镜头的方式，再现其诗歌情景。例如，"床前明月光"，译文变成了 My room falls into a dead silence, in the dead of night, as the moonlight falls, through the window, into my room, onto the floor …（深更夜半之时，我的房间陷入死寂——月光，透过窗户，落入我的房间，照在屋里的地上），整整五个诗行，补译出许多细节。接下来的"疑是地上霜"却简单了：which seems to be frostily coated with a thin film（似乎着上一层薄薄的白霜）。"疑"，其实非"疑"，当解为"好像"之意，因此，seems to be 正好。"霜"，李白用作名词，英译却用其副词形式：frostily，可耐品味。

接下来，后两句的译文也多细节描写。"我本能地抬眼望，目光移开，落在月亮之上，而月亮之光，也照在我的身上。"想起李白"相看两不厌"的诗句来。汉语回译"思乡之情再次缠绕着我"，则想起邓丽君《千言万语》中的歌词："不知道为了什么，忧愁它围绕著我。"

望月之 67：A Roomful of Light & an Eyeful of Moon（满屋的月光，满眼的月亮）

读英文

She's **quite an eyeful**!
她真是个美人！

I **keep my eyes pinned on her**.
我的眼睛直勾勾地盯着她。

Inwardly she was running with a troubled tide of thought.
她内心里奔腾着愁苦的思潮。

I bowed my head and **thought of my far-off home**.
我低头想起我远方的家。

I dreamed of **my old home** last night.
昨晚我梦见我的老家了。

英文散译

A Roomful of Light & an Eyeful of Moon

My room is flooded with silvery light which seems to coat the bedside floor with a thin film of frost, whose source is traced upward to a bright moon peeping through the window — she is quite an eyeful! When I keep my eyes pinned on the moon, inwardly I am running with a troubled tide of thought, and I bow my head, to think of my far-off old home ....

英文诗译

A Roomful of Light & an Eyeful of Moon

My room is flooded with
silvery light which seems to
coat the bedside floor with a thin
film of frost, whose source is
traced upward to a bright moon
peeping through the window
— she is quite an eyeful!
When I keep my eyes pinned
on the moon, inwardly I am
running with a troubled tide of
thought, and I bow my head, to
think of my far-off old home ....

回译

满屋的月光，满眼的月亮
我的卧室里，溢满
着银色之光，似乎
将床前的地面
镀上了一层薄霜。
求其源，一轮明月，
正窥视窗户——
月亮，她是个美人！
当我直勾勾地盯着
月亮，内心里奔腾
着愁苦的思潮，
于是我低头，想起
我远方的老家……

译人语

译诗标题 *A Roomful of Light & an Eyeful of Moon*（《满屋的月光，满眼的月亮》），不是《静夜思》之文字，却是《静夜思》之情思，极写静夜思之深、之沉、之厚、之实。

译文中，"一轮明月，正窥视窗户"（a bright moon peeping through the window），乃逆向思维：从屋外到屋里，视角变化而已。

最后两个英文句子中，my far-off home 与 my old home，两者合并：my far-off old home（我远方的老家），正可表达"低头思故乡"之"故乡"。倒数第四行开始的译文：inwardly I am running with a troubled tide of thought, and I bow my head, to think of my far-off old home ….（内心里奔腾着愁苦的思潮，于是我低头，想起我远方的老家……）借鉴英文而来，译文地道、细腻、生动。

望月之 68：A Homey Reverie in Silvery Moonlight （银色月光中，家乡的遐想）

读英文

It's such a nice, **homey** name.
它是多么美好，温馨的一个名字啊。

Your apartment feels **homey**.
你的公寓有家的感觉。

You **glance up at me, then glance off toward** the clouds.
你抬眼看我，然后看着天上的云彩。

His black **hair was threaded with silver**.
他的黑发中夹杂着银发。

He reads my answer in my gaze, his torment **keeps growing** and his voice rises.
他从我的眼中读出了答案，其痛苦不断增长，声音不断提高。

He plunges her into a hug that nearly leaves her out of breath.
他使劲拥抱着她，几乎让她喘不过气来。

The rejection **plunged** her into the dark depths of despair.
遭到拒绝，使她陷入了绝望的深渊。

She **fell into a reverie about her childhood**.

她沉浸在对童年往事的遐想中。

When you dream, you've dropped **out of reality** into your own mental world.

当你在做梦的时候，你脱离现实，进入自己的精神世界。

英文散译

A Homey Reverie in Silvery Moonlight

I glance down at the strange floor, frostily white with a beam of silvery moonlight to set off my hair threaded with silver, before my strange bed, then glance off toward the moon which keeps waxing as my homesickness keeps growing — and I am plunged into a homey reverie about my childhood that nearly leaves me out of reality.

英文诗译

A Homey Reverie in Silvery Moonlight

I glance down at the strange
floor, frostily white with a
beam of silvery moonlight
to set off my hair threaded
with silver, before my strange
bed, then glance off toward
the moon which keeps waxing
as my homesickness keeps
growing — and I am plunged
into a homey reverie about
my childhood that nearly
leaves me out of reality.

回译

银色月光中，家乡的遐想
我目光下垂，看着
陌生床前的陌生地面：

霜白的银色月光，

映衬着我银丝的

头发；然后，看着

天上的月亮，渐渐

盈满，我的乡愁

也不断增长——

我陷入家乡的遐想

之中：想着我的童年，

我开始脱离现实，

插上飞翔的翅膀。

译人语

译文中，I glance down at the strange floor, frostily white with a beam of silvery moonlight to set off my hair threaded with silver, before my strange bed（我目光下垂，看着陌生床前的陌生地面：霜白的银色月光，映衬着我银丝的头发），两用 strange，想起王维诗句"独在异乡为异客"的英译：as a stranger in a strange land。其实，《静夜思》当有如此之人生况味。另外，"映衬着"（to set off），也是译者的遐想：月光如银，白发如银——人世之沧桑矣。因而，故乡在我的心里，便愈发亲切起来。"看着天上的月亮，渐渐盈满，我的乡愁也不断增长"（glance off toward the moon which keeps waxing as my homesickness keeps growing），英译中两用 keep，再次产生了我和月亮之间的互动。想起一首歌曲，名字就叫《月亮走我也走》："月亮走我也走，我送阿哥到村口。"这里却是：月亮满，我也满；月亮满满的光，我心满满的愁，满满的乡愁。

最后三行："想着我的童年，我开始脱离现实，插上飞翔的翅膀。"（a homey reverie about my childhood that nearly leaves me out of reality.）回译中，添加了"插上飞翔的翅膀"，而英文却无需如此表述。

望月之 69：Moonlit Night & Moonlit Thoughts（月照之夜·月照之思）

读英文

Her entire face glows beautifully.
她的整个脸庞都容光焕发，很是好看。

The sun **keeps beaming on my face**.
阳光不停照在我的脸上。

I **lifted my eyes and stared at** the vaulted ceiling.
我抬起头，盯着拱形的天花板。

Pleasure seems **impossible without the constant input of** pain.
没有无尽之痛苦，便没有快乐可言。

She will **pass the night** there.
她会在那儿过夜。

Our thoughts are with their family and friends.
我们总想着他们的家人和朋友。

英文散译

Moonlit Night & Moonlit Thoughts

The bedside floor seems to glow with a thin film of frost, and my entire face glows wistfully, as the moon keeps beaming through the window, into the room, onto the ground, and on my face. I lift my eyes toward the moon and, with the constant input of moonlight, nostalgia seems possible. How shall I pass the moonlit night when my moonlit thoughts are flying homeward, to be with my dear family members?

英文诗译

Moonlit Night & Moonlit Thoughts

The bedside floor seems to glow

with a thin film of frost, and my

entire face glows wistfully, as the

moon keeps beaming through the

window, into the room, onto the

ground, and on my face. I lift my eyes

toward the moon and, with the

constant input of moonlight, nostalgia

seems possible. How shall I pass

the moonlit night when my moonlit

thoughts are flying homeward, to

be with my dear family members?

回译

月照之夜·月照之思
床前的地上，似乎
闪烁着一层薄霜，
我的整个脸庞闪烁着
思念之光，月亮不停
照着——穿过窗户，
进入卧室，落在地上，
照我脸上。我抬头
看着月亮：随着月光
的不断注入，乡愁

渐生。我该如何度过
这月照之夜？——
当我的月照之思
向家飞翔，想着
和我亲爱的家人
团聚，共度美好时光。

译人语

译诗标题 *Moonlit Night & Moonlit Thoughts*（月照之夜&月照之思），具现代散文之美。译文中，the moon keeps beaming through the window, into the room, onto the ground, and on my face（月亮不停照着——穿过窗户，进入卧室，落在地上，照我脸上），介词的运用较好：through，into，onto，on，可谓发挥了英文善用介词的优势；回译对应汉语："穿过"、"进入"、"落在"、"照"等，显然不如英文之形象。

倒数第六行开始：with the constant input of moonlight, nostalgia seems possible（随着月光的不断注入，乡愁渐生），此句之添加，极富诗意。倒数第三行中，两个 moonlit，呼应诗题。回译最后的"共度美好时光"，乃添加成分，却也合情合理。另外，英文译诗 12 行，回译却变成了 15 行。从《静夜思》到英文译诗，再从英文译诗到汉语回译，字、词、句、行等，都需要灵活变通，一切以诗情诗感为重心。

望月之 70：The Most Luminous Moon: a Melting Heart (月之灿兮：琴心柔肠)

读英文

His heart melted when he saw the little girl crying.
看到这个小女孩哭起来，他的心软了。

My heart freezes, and my brows furrow instantly.
我的心僵住了，我的眉毛也顷刻之间皱了一下。

A gust of wind made the candles **flare**.
一阵风吹得烛光摇曳。

The fire **flared** out brightly.
火光闪亮。

I **raised my gaze to meet hers** and glared.
我抬起头，去迎合她的目光，闪烁着亮光。

I dropped my gaze and instantly knew she wouldn't be walking on that foot anymore tonight.
我垂下目光，立刻知道，今晚她不会再用那只脚走路了。

The greatest pleasure can only exist in the context of the most terrible pain.
只有最大的痛苦，才有最大的快乐。

英文散译

The Most Luminous Moon: a Melting Heart

My heart freezes at the sight of a floorful of frosty film of rime, the source of which is traced to the luminous object flaring through the window. I raise my gaze to meet hers, then drop it with a melting heart — the greatest homesickness can only exist in the context of the most luminous moon in such a night of dead silence.

英文诗译

The Most Luminous Moon: a Melting Heart

My heart freezes at the sight

of a floorful of frosty film

of rime, the source of which

is traced to the luminous

object flaring through

the window. I raise my gaze

to meet hers, then drop it

with a melting heart —

the greatest homesickness can

only exist in the context

of the most luminous moon

in such a night of dead silence.

回译

月之灿兮：琴心柔肠

我的心僵住了，

当我看到地上

全是一层霜白

之光——追根

求源，只见一个

发光的物体，闪窗

而入。我抬起头，

去迎合其光；

然后，垂下目光：

乡思浓。在这样

一个死寂的晚上，

月之灿兮，琴心柔肠。

译人语

前两个英文句子中，描写 heart 的动词，一个 melt（融化；消散），一个 freeze（冻结；僵硬），正好是反义词。见地面之霜而 freeze，抬头见月而 melt；一个暗示游子独在异乡生活之艰难，一个联想到月是故乡明，月是故乡圆。

英译中，"地上"一般译为 ground 或 floor，这里采用 floorful，构成明显的头韵：a floorful of frosty film of rime，音韵效果明显。动词 flare 的使用，也出人意表之外。英文例子中表示"烛光摇曳"或"火光闪亮"，译文中，the luminous object flaring through the window（一个发光的物体，闪窗而入），意象鲜明。然后，I raise my gaze to meet hers（我抬起头，去迎合其光），月光含情——重在我之多情：多情，而移情矣。

最后一句最堪回味：the greatest homesickness can only exist in the context of the most luminous moon in such a night of dead silence。借鉴英文之后，附加介词短语 in such a night of dead silence，更添一层余味。汉语回译："在这样一个死寂的晚上，月之灿兮，琴心柔肠。"以简驭繁。中文无法再现英文之美，英文难传汉诗之情。为什么国人也喜欢阅读古诗英译？欲察其如何在另一种语言中变化、折腾。由是，英译古诗，别样情，带给读者另一种审美体验和感动。

望月之 71：A Welter of Thoughts Under the Midnight Moon（午夜月下：缭乱的思绪）

读英文

The sun was setting **in a welter of crimson** behind the hill.
山后一片红色，太阳正在落山。

The late afternoon sun slanted down in the yard.
傍晚的太阳斜照到院子里。

The warmth of the April day was ebbing into a faint but balmy chill.
四月温暖的日子，变得微凉而令人慰藉。

I have just cleared up **a bewildering welter of** data saved in my computer.
我刚整理了保存在我电脑里的数据，这些数据杂乱无章、很难处理。

The plantation clearings and **miles of cotton fields smiled up to a warm sun, placid, complacent**.
种植园的空地和几英里的棉花地，晒在温暖的太阳下，平静而满足。

英文散译

A Welter of Thoughts Under the Midnight Moon

The late night moonlight slants down through the window, into the room, onto the ground, lending a frosty, silvery coat to the floor, when the warmth of the broad daylight has already ebbed, and is ebbing into a faint but balmy chill under the moon, which reduces me to a bewildering welter of thoughts heavily tinctured with homesickness, and in my mind's eye, miles after miles of fields upon fields are smiling up to a brilliant moon, placid, complacent.

英文诗译

A Welter of Thoughts Under the Midnight Moon

The late night moonlight slants down

through the window, into the room,

onto the ground, lending a frosty, silvery

coat to the floor, when the warmth of

the broad daylight has already ebbed,

and is ebbing into a faint but balmy chill

under the moon, which reduces me

to a bewildering welter of thoughts

heavily tinctured with homesickness,

and in my mind's eye, miles after miles

of fields upon fields are smiling up

to a brilliant moon, placid, complacent.

回译

午夜月下：缭乱的思绪

深夜的月亮，斜照，

穿窗，进入卧室，落在

地上，给地面镀上一层

如霜之银白。此刻，

大白天的温暖，早已

褪去；月亮之下，一切

都变得微凉而令人慰藉。

我的思想，不觉缭乱

起来；乡愁，渐生渐浓。

心眼所及，千里百里，
田野片片，沐浴在月光
之下：平静，祥和。

译人语

英文句子中，两个含有 welter，在 in a welter of crimson 和 a bewildering welter of data 中，welter 都做名词用，大意为："杂乱的一堆；一片混乱；翻滚；起伏"。还可以做动词用，意为"翻滚；沉迷；混乱"。例如：Mother told her son not to welter in pleasure and idleness（妈妈告诫儿子，不要沉溺于享乐和闲逸）。英译中，welter 使用两次，标题中出现一次，然后诗中：a bewildering welter of thoughts（我的思想，不觉缭乱起来）——《静夜思》之思，不过如此。另外，译文中的语言亮点，还有 ebb 的两次使用，heavily tinctured with homesickness 等，都是读英文借鉴而来。